Cover designed by www.behance.net/kategunia
Special thanks to Glynis Pryce Milburn

TOM SCOTT'S LAD

George Scott

For My Family

CHAPTER I

My first real memory takes me back to the war years, more years than I care to remember really, and goes some way to explaining why I was a constant source of worry to my mother. I must have been two or three years old and I was lying in a large bed, at the bottom of my bed (or as it turned out, my Mother's bed) stood a number of people, maybe five or six, I couldn't see their faces as the only light in the room must have been from the glow of candles. They were obviously looking at the small figure in the bed and were talking in murmurs so as not to disturb what they thought was a sleeping child. I remember one of them saying quietly "I think he is awake." A man detached himself from the huddle and a very cold hand was placed on my brow.

Many years later I found out that the man was Doctor Goldsborough and the rest of the mysterious group that had stood in the glow of the candles that night were my relatives. They had been sent for by my Mother and Grandmother fearing I would not live until the following day due to a serious case of yellow jaundice. Incidentally, my relatives had clubbed together and bought me a little green and yellow truck that I had eyed enviously for weeks each time I had gone past Minnie Davel's shop. I would lean against the window and look longingly at this wonderful tin plate toy but now wonder, through the passing of time, where that little truck went? However, I doubt the illness was worth a green and yellow tin plate toy because, as many things in childhood, it simply disappeared without trace.

My name is George, Scotty to my childhood friends, but in my youth, I was usually referred to as: "I know your Dad, you're Tom Scott's Lad! Just you wait till I've had a word with him!" or words to that effect. I don't suppose I was an exceptionally bad kid, but in the post war world of no electricity, no TV, no expendable income and one battery operated radio, you had to make your own entertainment and earn your pennies as and when you could find them. Living in a particularly small town, everyone knew everyone else's business and the goings on in and around Wigton were the equivalent of today's soap operas.

Tom Fisher the Barber had an establishment which was situated in, what at one time, had been his or the previous property owners, front room. This was a hotbed of much gossip and goings-on (not that any of the menfolk would admit to relishing in a good bit of gossip you understand...). Two walls were taken up with large wooden settles covered in brown stuff that looked like leather and may well have been in those far off days, always polished to a high degree and, for young boys, was rather uncomfortable. Short legs and short pants meant you either stuck to the leather with sweat or slid off because of the polished surface.

Under these two large pieces of furniture nestled about half a dozen spittoons filled with sawdust and woe betide any child when called to the haircutting chair if they managed to upset one of these receptacles. Then the talk would revolve around how clumsy and feckless this new generation was, with obviously no thought for their elders, never listened to good advice and most of all how they all, without exception, got up to all kinds of mischief. Nor would any of them own up when in bother. Not at all like them when they were bairns. Often regaling of the kick up the backside or clatter of their ears they would have got, even though they never did anything wrong, how times had changed!

Tom was the local sage and any new gossip, misdeeds or just anything out of the ordinary would reach him before anywhere else. As with all sages he had his regulars, not always in for a haircut or shave, but to just drop by and exchange the latest news, even if most of it was second or third hand. Possibly someone had an injury and his or her arm in a sling at one end of the town, by the time it reached the barbers shop the whole arm had had to be removed. Such as news was, and possibly still is today.

Tom was always happy to listen to how much hair was to be removed or what style was required but he made no difference to any of his customers young or old, everyone got the kind of haircut that Tom liked, almost bald! He always said he gave good value for money and no frills.

Us young ones had to sit on a board precariously placed across the arms of the barber's chair where fidgeting brought a quick response from the man with the scissors. "If you don't sit still I'll cut one of your bloody ears off." Or words to that effect and it always worked. The one thing I remember most about Tom was that his specs would gradually slide down his nose and at the very last minute he would rescue them with his middle finger. This movement was always accompanied with a deep sniff. How he always managed to save his specs will remain a mystery and how he always managed to avoid poking out one of his eyes with his scissors, that he never put down, will remain the same.

Most parts of the little town were known by nicknames rather than their proper ones, such as Back Way, Vinegar Hill, The Rabbit Warren and to be honest most of the men and boys were also known by their nicknames instead of, as they say, their given names. Bant, Young Bant, Billy Bant, Bant frae Fletcher toon, Milky, Patch, Young Patch, Patchy, Bloss, Apple, Blow, Pin head, Tut-too, Crutch, Twin (both lads were given this name regardless of which one was being referred to), Electric hare, Bomber, Grip, Whiskers, Buff. An endless array of nick names but not one of them carried any offence. All these names bring back a face almost instantly, however a mention of the same person by their given name would require more than a little brain searching. Most of these people would stay around the town for the rest of their lives and would appear from time to time. It was a little strange that in such a small town it could be months or longer without seeing a particular lad but would always remember one another with a greeting of some kind. Often a ribald remark, sometimes a bit of gallows humour, such as: "still with us then" or, more likely "Hey Scotty been away? Never missed you till now." Invariably followed by a chuckle.

The swimming baths to a small snotty nosed boy was a great draw. For a few pennies I could spend the afternoon with pals. The few pennies were a problem and early on I found out why I had Grandparents. By sitting on my Grandma's McPherson's couch looking as miserable, dejected and unkempt as possible with only a grunt or an "eh" in reply to any questions put my way, feet swinging barely touching the ground, socks around my ankles, shoes with barely a trace of polish, eventually the right question was asked "What are you doing this afternoon?". My quick response would be "I was going to the baths, but Mam hasn't any money." Then the offer of money for the baths was always preceded with "you can't go looking like that, get your face washed and come here till I comb your hair, what a mess." Taking me by the collar of my jacket my Gran would shuffle me about trying with little success to make me look tidy. Amazing what a little boy will put up with for the price of a ticket for the baths. I remember once I got outside my Gran's house I would wriggle about and run my fingers through the now tidy hair to achieve the previous unkempt look.

The Caretaker of the baths was called Albert Haney. It wasn't until many years later I discovered Albert was the one person at the baths who couldn't swim. If, unfortunately, anyone was to get into trouble while in the pool all Albert had was a long pole with a big scoop on the end that was normally used to swill down the walkway around the edge. Luckily, I never heard of anyone being in such a predicament as most kids in the town could swim. Probably due to being thrown in and made to, even if it was just the dog paddle.

The diving steps at the deep-end of the pool (now removed), along with the steps to the viewing balcony (and usually the balcony itself too), were used by a lot of lads to show how macho they were. Macho may not be the word in those days more like show-offs. Daring exploits as they jumped, dived and ran from the various heights into the pool. Now, when I look at the height of the ceiling where the balcony and the changing cubicles were, they were daring indeed, as the water was only six feet at the deepest part. Although the worst injury I can remember anyone ever getting, was at most a few scrapes and some dignity damage.

Albert was a little carefree and some of the lads would wait until he was busy with something in the boiler room then simply walk into the changing room, get changed and straight into the pool as if they belonged there. I am sure Albert knew what was going on, but it was too much bother to go through all the arguments, one way and another this guy was a bonus to the town. Should you be unfortunate enough not to have trunks or towel, for a couple of pennies they could be hired, they were probably from the lost property but did come in very useful.

At the time hardly any of the townspeople would have had a bath in their homes and many of them would use, what was known as, the slipper baths, which were located at the swimming pool. I have absolutely no idea why they were called slipper baths, but they would frequent the baths on a weekly, fortnightly or monthly basis. The slipper baths were made from cast- iron and so deep a young boy could not see over the side. The bonus was there was no restriction as to how much hot water you could use.

However, for most it would be a tin bath in front of the fire, to be used by as many of the family as possible because hot water was a rare commodity. Should the used water still have any warmth left, it would be used for washing clothes or maybe the kitchen floor. Nothing ever went to waste.

There was never any finesse in learning how to swim, as soon as it was realised that you were not able, a couple of the bigger lads would simply take an arm and a leg each and on a count of three you were simply hurled into the middle, and, just to make sure, when you finely scrambled out they would do the same thing again. After a few replays, the first few strokes came naturally and on seeing you could now manage you were simply left to get on with it. I can't say I felt the same elation as when I learned to ride a bike, but it is certainly up there with some of the better things I have managed to achieve.

At the time I did not understand why Albert would shout at the lads who seemed to take a long time clambering out of the water by the cubicles used by the girls as changing facilities. It was only when I got older I came to realise that the cubicle doors didn't reach the ground by at least a foot and a half.

After swimming at the local baths most of the lads and a few of the more tomboy girls would gather on the steps to the entrance to decide what was next! Those with a few pence would head for the chip shop, some would head off home or into town, maybe one or two would head off in the direction of Tenters, Market Hill or maybe have a ratch on the tip at East end.

CHAPTER 2

The tip was a big draw to me as, with a bit of luck, I might find a few jam jars. The one -pound size was worth a penny, the two pound size or a Domestos bottle was worth a massive tuppence. Small lemonade bottles brought a halfpenny, the large ones a penny. The receptacles were invariably covered in ash and who knows what other detritus but, undaunted, they would be taken to a nearby spring to be washed.

The only downside to my excursions to the ash tip was the men that worked on the ash cart. It was a wise thing to keep an ear open for the old wagon churning its way up the ash path that lead from the road. On the rare occasion that the sound of the engine was missed there was always a big to do. The wagon would pull up to the edge of the dump, where it normally disgorged its contents, the crew would make all sorts of dire threats and would set of in mock pursuit of any offenders. "Do you want to catch a disease or something, go on bugger off and don't come back." For some reason, the ash car men always knew my parents, using the age old "I know who your dad is" and so on. I never waited to see if any of them would be fast enough to catch me; the words were enough for now. I don't know how these guys coped; the wagon was no bigger than a modern delivery van and served the whole town. Everything had to be hand loaded; God knows what was in some of the bins. It was not unusual to find dead animals or rotten fish teaming with maggots and flies, as this wagon was the only way for householders to get rid of their waste and believe me, what was counted as waste, was waste indeed.

On a good day I could collect enough money to gain entrance to Joe Cusack's picture house, The Palace, or the flea pit as it was locally known. Who knows? On a good day of rummaging I may even have earned enough for a bag of Stuart Watson's chips too. I will never know how I did not catch some of the diseases the ash car men referred to? Or at least something that would lead to, at the very least, a week off school? But here I still am, all these years on.

It was sometimes worth a look in the rubbish that Robert and John Scott, (no relation), dropped at the tip. They cleaned out the towns drains; the cart they used was not unlike half a giant oil drum on wheels, drawn by the same old horse they used to deliver coal to the gas works. I am sure the horse knew where the drains were because as soon as one drain was emptied, and the lid replaced the horse would lean into its harness and quietly pad on to the next one without so much as being asked. The gunge they eventually dumped at the tip could, occasionally, contain the odd coin and with the help of a stick, a little probing could prove worthwhile. Always remembering to keep out of sight until the two men departed because, they too, would give short shrift same as the ash car men.

My perpetual quest for pin-money was supplemented by the acquisition of goods in kind. Nowadays such things as sweets, cakes, sugar, dried fruit and chocolates can be picked up easily in every shop and supermarket in unlimited quantity, but as a boy these items were a rare treat. Firstly, because they were rationed and secondly, they were expensive. Three 2oz coupons (50g) were issued per month for sugar and sweets, which is the equivalent of about three Mars Bars a month. For a sweet toothed, growing lad, this was a harsh existence indeed, especially when you needed both coupons AND money for your sugary fix. I soon learned where I could acquire additional pennies and coupons, just to keep me going and I even cultivated my own supply of titbits from top secret sources!

One of these sources was Munny McPherson, my grandmother, who was a confectioner. After I started school her place of work had to be visited daily. After the bell went to notify everyone it was the end of lessons I would head off to McGuffey's Bakery to investigate what goodies had suffered damage during the course of being prepared for sale in the shop. It is entirely possible that this time of my life had something to do with my pleasure in all things pastry or confection. Even today I blame the owners of the shop for my love of pies and cakes, as it was at their insistence that maybe I would like to eat this or that damaged delight. In fact, looking back, I am surprised that I am not obese.

Maybe they felt sorry for this scrawny lad in short trousers that would wear a tank top, baggy shirt with his socks around his ankles and daily prop up the door jamb at teatimes, shuffling from foot to foot or with ankles crossed as if to try and hide the baggy socks. However, I do feel that I did in my own small way help them out with what, after all would have eventually fed someone's pigs or chickens. As with the jam jars and bottles, recycling is nothing new, is it?

From McGuffey's I would accompany my Grandmother (Munny) home to New Street. This street in those far distant days was really a complete community all on its own with a number of shops, a garage, an ironmonger and butchers.

There was also a dentist where my pals and I, on a nice day, would sit with our backs to the wall opposite the front door and take a great deal of pleasure in watching the poor unfortunates going in. Some reached the door and did an immediate turn around as if they had forgotten something they needed to do elsewhere. The interesting part was the door opening and the casualties leaving as fast as their legs would carry them almost always with a handkerchief or bandage clasped to their mouths. Nothing to laugh about, but it was top entertainment for us, although we only laughed when we were sure they were not watching us. Some were known to shake their fists if they happened to see us sniggering and one or two even took a deliberate step in our direction just to spoil our fun.

New Street was also a short cut for thousands of sheep driven from Hopes Auction to the Railway Station. Every Tuesday these black-faced sheep would hurtle past my Grandmothers lane jumping and bouncing like little nervous woolly dervishes. The occupants of all the properties would make sure their doors if not closed, were closely guarded, usually by the lady of the house as it was not unusual to find one of these woolly creatures taking sanctuary inside any open door.

Wigton auction was known for many miles around and was a big draw for many of the lads about my own age. The auction was not simply for sheep and cattle but specialised in the sale of horses, as most heavy work on the farms and many other enterprises was done by these magnificent animals.

The horse sales were something to behold, tractors were just making their way onto farms at this time and the need for heavy horses was, without anyone realising it, in decline in a big way, the 1950's found masses of these horses at Hopes auction. A couple of times a year along with other sales such as the sale of land and dispersal sales was the horse sales, held during the Spring and again in the Autumn these could last for three or more days at a time. Dozens of these huge working animals would be sold along with riding mounts and cart ponies. Unfortunately, some were bought to send to the continent for meat. Willing lads could make a few pennies if they weren't scared of these giant, but usually quiet equines. Lads hardly reaching up to the animal's belly would earn up to a shilling a day by leading them on halters, one in each hand, down to the railway station where they would be loaded into wagons for their journey to who knows where?

Sunday mornings around the Fountain, as it is known, brought out the local Salvation Army band led by Jack McGee and his squeeze box with all the well-known Salvation Army songs. Some of the less inebriated, from the Saturday night surfeit of ale in one or other of the local taverns of which there were many, would stand against the shop windows and pretend to listen. The collection box brought an altogether different attitude from the audience and they would disappear as smoke does in a breeze. Jack sang the good song and preached to anyone daft enough or unwise enough to let him.

Through the week Jack would sit on the edge of his horse cart and be around the countryside to gather scrap or old rags which, somehow, he managed to turn into beer money. His tiny wife would run alongside the horse, if things were not going so well or there wasn't much in the way of business and Jack would crack his whip and call 'Gid up theer', sometimes it was difficult to tell if he was whipping the horse or Jane as they both would quicken their pace.

It wasn't unusual, as a lad, to be out in the countryside and come across Jane with a handcart or an old pram full of scrap iron or an old mangle as she headed home at a jog, always wearing a bonnet, scarf and overcoat, of unknown age or origin, that was usually held together with string; odd socks and stockings with a pair of galoshes meant for someone with feet at least twice as big as her own. She tolerated this for years probably as she knew nothing else, and I think she probably missed her husband when he died. She lived for quite a few years after Jack's demise but still dressed the same and could be seen on occasion in the town shuffling around the market or the auction mart, and almost always with her old pram.

CHAPTER 3

Motor vehicles were not numerous in my formative years, but I can remember being run over twice in the same day. Small weans like myself used a short-cut from New Street through Moore's Garage down a steep ramp onto Station Road; partly to prove how brave we were as the mechanics would shout various abusive words with endless threats about next time when they caught one or other of us, and the dire consequences that awaited, of course they all knew my dad too. I would sneak quietly across the New Street end of the garage watching to see if there was anyone about before running down the wooden ramp that joined the upper floor in New Street to the lower floor in Station Road hoping that the sliding door was not bolted. When it was, this gave the mechanics an unfair advantage and allowed them to fetch you a clout around the ear or a kick up the backside.

The day I was run over or rather dragged down the street started out well enough with my sneaking to the top of the ramp and, goodness me, not only was the sliding door not bolted but it was wide open with the mechanic outside probably putting petrol in a customer's car. Down the ramp at full speed and out the sliding door, bang, into the side of a passing car. Cars in those days had door handles facing front and my elbow just fitted between the handle and the bodywork. Off I went trailing alongside the car. I was dragged down the road for some distance before someone shouted and alerted the driver that he had an unwanted passenger. I don't remember what happened next but apparently, as soon as I was unhitched from the car I shot off like a greyhound before the driver could ascertain if

I was alright or before he could give me a clout for running into his vehicle. Later on, that same day, the bruises and shock forgotten, an almost identical incident happened, only this time the door handle didn't connect, and I simply bounced off the side of the motor. I am almost certain that one of the workers had been keeping an eye out as before I could gain my feet he had me by the scruff of the neck, all I could see was the horror in the man's eyes. "You alright lad?" I had no intention of getting to know this man as I was sure I would be in big trouble when all this came to light. I struggled and fought, all the time the man was saying "Hold still, you will be alright let's have a look see if there isn't any damage." I wasn't for holding still and wriggled some more, my jacket gave way and I was free, the mistake I made was in heading for the ramp and home. There was a problem half way up the ramp, in the shape of Mr. Stamper. The mechanic was close behind with my jacket; my escape had been short lived. Should I have made my escape I would have been clear and free. But Mr Stamper just happened to know who I was.

It was Mr. Stamper who led the delegation to my Grandmother McPherson's house. There was no escape. A couple of sharp raps on number nineteen's door brought her to, what I thought would be, my rescue, but when I saw her face my heart sank. I hung like a wet rag in the hands of Mr. Stamper as my escapade was told to my Grandmother. Her expression became more and sterner as the tale unfolded. Taking me firmly, but in a gentle way, she informed the small group it had taken to quell this little reprobate, that it was alright to leave me in her hands and she would deal with it. I don't think the way my grandmother dealt with the situation was what the small crowd would have expected.

"Are you all right lad? There's nothing broken is there? Any cuts or bruises? Just look at that graze on your elbow. I don't know what we are going to do with you my lad. If you carry on like this you are going to get yourself killed. Come on let's get some of that muck off and see how bad it is."

My grandmother's cure-all then was a pale yellow liquid in a bottle it was called TCP and must have been good for whatever ailed anyone as not only did it sting like blazes it smelled terrible and the smell lasted for days.

My family's name for it was Tom Cat's Pee. And that just about summed it up.

After a quick dab on all the exposed injuries with her cure for everything from ear-ache to boils, the table was set, and tea and cake administered both in large quantities, this was her next best thing as a cure. It worked instantly on a small boy with such injuries. Nothing was said to the rest of the family and the incident was put to one side and forgotten between my best friend and me.

CHAPTER 4

Money to a small boy was always a problem, and most times there was nothing at all to be done about the situation. But now and then, maybe not too honestly, it was possible to scrape a few pennies together and a little excitement as well.

For some time, I don't know exactly how long, I stayed with my Grandmother and Aunt in their small one and a half downstairs rooms and a large bedroom upstairs. It did have an outside toilet laid on, which of course was shared with neighbours and if you were quick you never noticed the cold in winter. Being small, the house didn't take a lot of heating but I remember my breath used to freeze in beautiful patterns on the glass panes and they stayed frozen all day, sometimes for days at a time. I was spoiled there and enjoyed being spoiled rotten. Sugar and sweets particularly were a rare thing and still only available with coupons. I was lucky because during the war and for a good number of years after, both my Gran, and my aunt got used to going without both, so it was down to me to use their coupons as well as my own, but of course there was the other little problem, funds, or rather the lack of same.

Noel Carrick was a popular figure probably because he owned a tobacco and sweet shop. I like to think we were friends because he would take time and assist with the choice of goodies, never in a hurry. Looking back now maybe he was the same with all his customers. Smasher bars, McCowan toffee bars, Barley sugar twists, rhubarb rock along with other tasty sweets lined up behind the glass counter purposely at the right height for a small boy to peruse. Because my Grandmother and aunt spoiled me I was a regular, and would be addressed with "What can I get you today Mr. Scott?" how was that for being important?

Of course I needed money to go with my coupons and being resourceful I acquired skills and schemes to secure the necessary ready cash. This ranged from sitting on the chair looking as if the world had forgotten me, hoping I would be noticed, tip diving, or to calling at Ties fish shop to see if they needed cleaned any of the old square tin boxes they used to pack their crisps in. These same boxes would be used many times over the years and some of them could be inches thick with gummed paper used to seal the contents, and from time to time would need the sticky residue removed. No elf and safety in those days. The contents were the first potato crisps I ever clapped eyes on, and any flavour could be purchased just as long as they were plain.

It was quite intriguing to watch the crisps made, after being peeled the potato was first cut very thinly with a thingamajig, before being dried in a wire basket and unceremoniously dumped in very hot fat. The roar from the cold sliced potatoes accompanied by clouds of steam was something to behold for a small boy sitting in a corner, more interested in what was going on than in the job at hand. Watching the steam condense on the windows and listening to the hiss of the frying crisps. "Have you not got those tins done yet?" A sharp reminder of why I was there, bringing me back to the job at hand. After spending the required amount of time in the hot fat, the crisps would be rescued with a large shovel like object full of holes then deposited in a basket similarly full of holes, where they would be shaken to remove the excess dripping (rendered beef fat) and left to cool.

The next process was to put a handful of the now cool crisps into a grease proof bag and seal it with a machine rather like an old-fashioned pencil sharpener, the bag was held closed at the top and wound through the small jaws which magically sealed the bag. Well, mostly it was closed; sometimes I had to do it two or three times before it was sealed properly. No such thing as weights and measures, just guess work and some customers would be lucky and some less so. The job was boring to me and contemplated only as a last resort.

A strange sight I will never forget happened when I was staying with my Grandmother Munny and Aunt Ginny when they lived in New Street. There was obviously a dispute going on and being a small boy, I wasn't privy to know about it. Probably teatime or thereabouts, there was an almighty commotion in the small kitchen that eventually spilled out into the parlour.

My Aunt Ginny was reversing through the doorway both arms raised as if to protect herself, she was followed by my Grandmother who was swinging a raw, whole herring I think! As the fish descended on my Aunt, it was accompanied by expletives I didn't know my Gran knew. The words emphasised each stroke and each time there was a direct hit, pieces of the fish were strewn everywhere. The last intelligible words I remember were "Now tell me you don't want fish for tea!" My Aunt was the kind of person that could cause a fight in a telephone box. She just didn't know when to shut-up. It may have been a few days or even weeks later; I am not sure, but a similar incident, this time with a bowl of rice pudding, which caused me no end of mirth, as it was tipped over her head. As my Gran's eyes met mine that day she winked, turned around and went back to the kitchen leaving the dish upside down with the contents gradually dripping down on Ginny's shoulders and continuing down her dress, her shoes, to come eventually to a rest on the floor. On both these occasions I managed not to look in my Aunts eyes but to squeeze past her making my escape outside before bursting with laughter as I ran off down the lane. After saying this about my aunt she really had a heart of gold and would go out of her way to help.

Most of the pubs in the town belonged to the State Management - a company brought into being by the government to try and curtail the excesses of the demon drink, as most of the people in this part of the world were involved in manufacturing munitions of one kind or another, and the government did not want this manufacturing to be compromised by excessive drinking – so drinking time was under the control of the state management. But I digress! The beer bottles were all the same, being owned by the said State Management and these bottles commanded a penny on the return to the Pub. Some of the managers may have been a little careless and left the yard door open and crates of empty bottles unattended, so to speak, therefore it was possible for a young enterprising boy to slip unnoticed into the yard and quietly rescue a bottle or two, later to be taken to another pub in exchange for the penny deposit, and thereby allowing access to the pictures at a later stage. Like all good things, after a little while others of my age group learned about the system and it got out of hand, a nice little earner bit the dust. Time to move on.

Autumn was good in a lot of ways, it meant brambles were ripe and I could get paid sixpence a pound from Dicky Thornton, a man, who today would be called an entrepreneur, in those far off days he was a business man. He ran a garage, a taxi business, and would collect dead bodies after any accident, he had a metal lined coffin in a corner of his garage and at times I had seen him washing it out with a hose pipe, I thought better than to ask what he was doing.

My memory in my early days of Mr Thornton, to give him his proper title, was that he was a source of income from brambles to mushrooms and I have a lot to thank him for. Towards the end of the school holidays along with many from the community, I could afford those extra little items such as an extra visit to the cinema, or a visit to Noel Carrick's sweet shop when the goodies were available.

One such item was the coveted baseball boots in Johnsons shoe shop window. They drove me crazy and I would stick my nose against the glass each time I passed by, navy blue and white with great long laces, they were the bee's knees. If it had not been for Dicky Thornton I would never have been able to afford them, or maybe I should say my parents would not have been able to afford them, and they were worn to utter destruction before my mam could persuade me to throw them away. I don't remember ever getting another pair, but I did love them even as the soles departed from the uppers.

Along with the brambles it was also possible to gather rose hips, but they were only worth threepence a pound and besides the thorns were twice as big and caused no end of problems both with skin and shirt sleeves. Barbed wire was another problem for a youngster's trousers and this was where my aunt Ginny became very useful, she was a seamstress at Redmayne's tailors in Station Road. Ginny could make a repair to my trousers so my mother would never notice, well at least not until the trousers were washed. I managed to placate her by saying "well mam that's been done for ages!" Did she believe me? I don't think so! But nothing more was said.

Apart from the usual tramping around the countryside, now and again on a good day a picnic might be mentioned. Not a picnic with everything packed carefully in a woven basket, more like everything in paper bags in a shopping bag, jam sandwiches, cheese or my favourite even to this day, soggy tomato the soggier the better. These squidgy succulents did not, of course, set off as soggy - it just happened en route to our destination. Usually it would be Springs Wood where a lot of the water used in the town bubbled up through sand and cascaded through masses of water cress eventually into a small beck where it then joined other little streams to eventually becoming Speet Gill. This little stream still meanders through the town, though not now used for drinking or washing.

The beck and the fields around Wigton were an endless source of adventure, fun and unknowingly an education of sorts. We knew where to find mushrooms, brambles, hazelnuts, cherries and where the beck was deep enough to swim etc. I realise now that it was also an endless source of worry for my Mother. She never knew just when I would arrive home with the backside ripped out of my trousers or wet through after falling into the beck. I would be covered in cuts from barbed wire or have parts of me damaged from falls etc. Upstream from Tenters, my home, there was a long wooded area of fir trees known locally as the Long Planting. These trees reached all the way from the beck to Kirklands Lonning. At the beck end and a little further upstream was a tall stand of beech trees and underneath the trees were a few scattered chicken runs. This turned out to be a no-go area, every time anyone went near the chicken runs an old guy appeared from nowhere and with a few choice words the intruder was told to "bugger off". It seemed that this person knew all the families in the area as his parting words were "I know your bloody Dad and he will deal with you". These words were ringing through the wood each time I made my escape without, by the way, looking to see if he was following. Many years later I learned that this small wood was used to breed fighting cocks, and that was why no-one was allowed anywhere near.

Downstream from the long planting there were the remains of what looked like old buildings. It was not for another forty years of so was I to discover what they were, or more to the point what they used to be. This was just the best place where kids could play without being chased away. There was a series of walls and a great sluice with a big iron wheel, huge trees with branches leaning over the beck and we used the branches to fix ropes enabling us to swing back and forward to the other side with the added risk of falling in. We would play set gaps (a local term for daring do), someone was chosen to lead, jumping back and forth over the beck, as time went by the risks got greater, such as swinging over the beck and letting go mid-stream in the hope of landing safely on the opposite bank. The older lads and lassies would manage but as the younger ones tried, it got more and more difficult for them, this resulted in great mirth from the older kids as each time one of the younger ones failed to make it across there would be roars of laughter when they splashed into the water. Not so funny when it was one of them as sometime happened. One case in particular when my next-door neighbour (a lad who was a little over weight) laughed his chops off when one of the young kids had fallen in after letting go of the rope to early. However, he was airborne still laughing and shouting "this is how you do it". Big gob was one of the words shouted at him just as the rope parted company with the branch. Everyone in the group thought it was hilarious but we all beat a hasty retreat as he fumbled his way out of the stream, wonderful what can happen unexpectedly.

CHAPTER 5

As I got a bit older, life got a bit easier as I was able to add an honest day's work to my fundraising schemes. My very first job started when I was about thirteen or so, I had the opportunity to get a newspaper round. The lad that had it was leaving school shortly so I had to get a move on. The vacancy was with Harvey Messenger's paper shop on King St. Now I am not saying there was any collusion but, at the time, I went to Sunday school at the Old Armoury and the Sunday school teacher was a certain Eric Messenger, Harvey's son! Maybe it was a coincidence but on that very Sunday I happened to be one of the few attendees, it was impossible to interrupt the service, so I had decided to be early and maybe lend a hand to put out the various books before anyone else arrived. I remember, during distributing the literature, asking Eric if he knew about the newspaper round and did he know if it was still available. I thought he wouldn't cotton on me being early and giving him a helping hand - the smile on his face told me he was not a thick as all that.

He couldn't promise anything but would enquire as soon as he saw his Dad. Another wait!

Nothing happened even though I hung about the front of the shop as often as I could, not a soul said anything. It was a week later and another Sunday, so I was back at Sunday school in a helping mode yet again. Nothing was said for ages and I began to think I might just have to mention it again. Once again I had not taken age or experience into account as I opened my mouth to broach the subject. Without looking up from what he was doing Eric simply said "If you are still interested in the paper round you need to call at the shop and see my dad tomorrow." Another wait, it must have been my age as all this waiting for things to happen was just not in my nature but I could do nothing at all about it, roll on tomorrow. The only trouble was that it would have to be after school, although maybe I could do a runner at dinner time I could do it if things went right and be back for afternoon register. Down to the canteen and as soon as possible down town to see Mr Messenger (Harvey Messenger had now taken on a new guise he was now Mr) after all he may well become my boss.

I hadn't told anyone about the paper round, not even my family, someone might mention it to a neighbour, or rival, not telling anyone might increase my chances.

The morning lessons dragged by but eventually the bell went for dinner time, I wasn't first in the queue at the canteen door, but I was in the first half dozen or so. The smell from the kitchens was always good even though I was in a hurry it smelled good. We weren't allowed into the hall until a teacher was present and today I am sure he knew I wanted to be away and he dawdled down the corridor. (We were not allowed out of school unless it was to go to the dentist or doctors.) What they didn't know about wouldn't hurt, it might hurt me in the morning if they found out, but if I got the paper round it would be worth it.

In a small town such as I lived there would always be someone to see anything going on that shouldn't be going on, that Monday was no different as I would find out when I got home.

Mr Messenger's daughter Audrey was behind the counter in the shop she looked up as the doorbell tinkled "You want to see dad." I simply nodded. She went to the back of the shop and leaned though a curtain draped over the door. All I heard was a quiet murmur of voices. Audrey turned and beckoned me behind the counter. "Dad's through there." She turned and went back to what she had been doing when I came in.

Harvey, sorry, Mr Messenger, almost always had a stern sort of look about him, rather like a teacher when a particular pupil was thought not to have been giving the subject his complete attention. Today he was rolling up unsold newspapers to be used instead of sticks to light his fire at home. "Sit down, sit down." That was all indicating to a chair with a nod of his head, his spectacles perched on the end of his nose. A collar and tie and a shiny suit completed his attire. He spoke kind of properly, not the usual local dialect. "I understand you would like to have the job as delivery boy, is that right?"

"Yes Mr Messenger." I thought that would be enough of an answer.

"Is that it then?"

"Well, I do know the town and where most people live Mr Messenger."

"Have you got a bicycle?"

"No sir but I have the use of one." A half-truth as I thought of my brother's bike.

"Eric says you're not a bad sort of lad so if you come in next Monday the lad that does the round now will show you, half past four don't be late."

"Thank you Mr Messenger. Don't worry I'll be here."

With that, I was standing outside the shop tingling with excitement and couldn't tell anyone until tea time as I had to get back to school for the register. Half walking, half running down Laurel Terrace past the swimming baths, now I needed to take care none of the teachers saw me returning. Through the old railings that surrounded the school grounds, along the embankment and, after a careful look across the playing field, I quickly joined the throng of kids playing games on the grass.

Done it! I have only gone and done it! It was only then that I realised I didn't even know how much the pay was for the job. Never mind, whatever it was I was sure I would put it to good use. I've got a job, kept going through my head but it would have to stay there until tea time.

I wonder if it was my just landing the paper round and my state of happiness but as I crossed the playing field there was a girl with blondish ginger hair. As I passed her by she smiled, and sort of half lifted her hand as if unsure as to whether she should wave or not. I half smiled in return before lowering my head, after all she was a girl and I wondered what my classmates would make of it seeing me wave at a girl?

Over the ensuing days, I must admit, I did notice her more often, sometimes in a corridor, sometimes outside on the playing field and each time I received the same little smile before she would turn and start talking to her pals. These sorts of passing meetings continued for some time but it was not until I had taken over the paper round that I ever managed to speak to her. I readily admit for a young lad it was hard to speak to girls especially if, like me, any spoken words simply tumbled from my mouth in unintelligible garble. Or was I in love?

I benefited from my paper round in lots of ways other than being paid for doing it, if I hadn't been able to borrow my brother's bike I just had to use shank's pony or maybe if Audrey had hers with her I could use that. A bit of leg work was deemed to be good for me or so my dad would say. "A bit of exercise never hurt anyone." After a couple of weeks, I began to work out short cuts, quick ways of getting around the town. Through a lane here, down a lonning there. I was starting to notice things, better keep an eye on this apple tree or that pear tree - there may be a few freebies on a windy day.

Another benefit, at first unseen, was that the girl who kept smiling at me while on the playing field or in a corridor, visited her Grandmother after school. I never found out if this was by chance or design, until one day I was almost finished my round as I came around the corner of Highmoor Tower and there she was.

What to do? I didn't have time to be embarrassed, she was too close to pretend I hadn't seen her. Ann saved the moment. "Do you want me to take the paper in for my grandma?"

I had the paper out of the bag in a flash. "I didn't know your grandma lived here." I held the folded newspaper out and as she took it I think I held on to it a bit longer than necessary.

A smile and she turned into the alley way and with a little wave was gone.

I would see Ann a few times each week at school but managed to see her almost every afternoon on my paper round. She would hold onto the handlebars of my bike or if I was on foot, she would stand close. It was probably a lot of rubbish we talked. What else would young people do? She would take her grandma's paper in for me and at times would hand me a little hand-written note. Always containing the latest abbreviations such as S.W.A.L.K. Or B.O.L.T.O.P. and on a couple of occasions I got a peck on the cheek. However, the relationship between us was going nowhere and as time passed we drew apart, not that we were ever together so to speak. But she was nice, and anyway I had things to do, like fishing, getting together enough money for all-sorts of necessary items of the time, possibly five Woodbine from Noel Carrick's sweet shop.

CHAPTER 6

As my memories comes flooding back, I begin my tale proper with my very first encounter with the immense power of steam. As a lad, as opposed to a teenager, now and then a thunderous old steam roller would appear in the town, it was used to roll in the gravel used in repairing the roads. After covering the street with hot tar the men employed by the council would scatter the gravel on top, using deft stokes of their shovels they could cover large areas in one movement obviously this acquired skill would have taken a long time to master but they made it look so simple. However, the driver of this hot steaming roller drew all the attention of the bystanders, and we kids were pushed to the rear of the crowd, always with the warning "You don't want squashed do you? Get back on the pavement." It obviously didn't matter if they themselves got squashed. They needed to be in the front of things just to make sure the job was being done properly, just the right amount of tar and the right thickness of gravel. The audience kept up a running commentary "Looks like he's missed a bit" or "He looks new to the job, wonder who showed him how to drive because he hasn't a clue." And so on. Mostly ribbing I suspect, but you couldn't be sure, as some of the spectators were proficient in all things except perhaps work!

Until the job was complete the great lumbering roller was parked up at night, usually at the east end of the town and with it was the living accommodation for the driver as he moved from place to place. This vehicle resembled an old wooden railway van and it contained all the amenities that would be needed while away from home. The man who looked after the road roller would spend more time on the road than with his family, even on weekends he would wander down to east end and make sure everything was ok. The burnished green paint and the sparkling polished steel was obviously a source of pride for Solomon, he spent half his life with an oily rag wiping any surface within reach. In fact, some of the burnished paintwork inside the cab was missing completely due to his continued polishing. Looking at this giant machine it was almost impossible to realise what his hobby was! Solomon was the man where you would take your watch to be repaired. I am not joking, from overseeing this lumbering, smoking, steaming piece of machinery weighing in at about ten tons to repairing small delicate pocket watches always seemed incredible to me.

Were the encounters with this roller, the smell of hot oil and steam to stay hidden in my mind and maybe influence me in years to come? The rumble of the steel-clad rollers and smaller steel-clad wheels on the trailer did bear at least a similar sound to the wheels on the steel tracks on the railway. I was always fascinated by these enormous engines and these had a far greater impact on the turn of my life than any education or formal schooling.

I was never one for school but one day in particular was not to be a favourite, even though it turned out to be one of my most memorable. It started just the same as any other day but it was soon to take a sharp decline.

"Scott take these papers to the headmaster and don't dawdle", Mr Warwick handed me a bunch of papers. "Right there and back and don't take all day."

"Yes sir," was my prompt reply. Mr Warwick was one of our better teachers as far as I was concerned but still a teacher and could, given reason, mete out punishment with the best of his fellows. Maths to some extent was lost on me - the standard stuff, tables, addition, division etc. was alright but when it came to using letters instead of numbers it was all Double Dutch.

Tucking the obviously valuable papers under my arm I headed for the door, "Scott carry the damned thing properly and get back here right away."

I untucked the papers which automatically decided to spread themselves on the floor, great amusement descended on the class at my expense. It couldn't get any worse, or so I thought, until it was as I bent down to retrieve the scattered sheets of paper Mr Warwick did the same and his head met mine in mid-bend.

"God damned idiot all I wanted was for you to get these to the headmaster. Leave them alone they were in order now look at them."

"But sir."

"Never mind "but sir", stand over there until I get them sorted."

I did as I was told and stood by the door.

I was sure I had got off lightly as I was handed the now sorted papers Mr Warwick leaned past me and opened the door. "Go on and hurry up."

That was it? No, it wasn't. As I escaped through the opening I managed to receive the customary clout behind my head. However, I managed to hold on to the documents as I scurried away before the possibility of a second blow.

Turning into the corridor along the hall I met the headmaster, (Mr Brogden), going the opposite way

"Sir." That was it that was all I managed to say."

"Don't bother me now boy go and wait outside my room."

He went past me his gown in full stretch behind him as he disappeared around the corner. If there had been any dust on the floor it would have followed in his wake.

On arrival at Mr. Brogden's office I found a couple of lads from the same year as myself, before I could ask the question "What are you two here for?" One of them asked me.

Feeling a little cocky I remarked that I was here with a bunch of papers for the headmaster and asked them "What are you doing here?"

"Smoking down by the beck, and they took the packet of fags as well. Worse still the fags belong to my mother, I was only going to smoke one, now I'll be in bother when I get home for pinching her tabs."

I was still smirking when Mr. Brogden arrived back. He could lay on with the cane but today I was merely the delivery boy.

Nothing was said as the door closed behind the head.

A few minutes later the voice crackled through the door. "Come in you lot."

We all looked at each other, the bravest of us reached for the door handle and pushed it open a few inches. "I haven't got all day come in." Mr. Brogden's voice was raised now maybe he was showing a little impatience. However, it must have been for the other two, I was only a messenger. So, as the other two went through the door I hesitated.

"You as well Scott, come on get in here."

That was the moment I suspected things were about to go wrong. "Excuse me sir I have just…" That was as far as I got.

The head looked up at the lad on my left. "Well are you dumb."

"No sir, Mr Postlethwaite sent us."

"Go on,"

"Larking about on the stairs sir."

Mr. Brogden pushed his chair back and stood up. As he turned towards the cupboard immediately behind him, I had a premonition of what was to come. It felt like I was becoming embroiled in something that had nothing to do with me, I needed to do something and quickly.

"Sir, I'm not with these lads."

"Too bad, right hold out your hands palm up."

We all looked at one another

I don't know how I finished up in the middle of all this but it was now or never. "Sir I haven't done anything Mr Warwick sent me with these papers." Saved, or so I thought.

"Put the papers on the desk."

I did as I was requested and felt relieved. The feeling lasted about a second.

"Now hold out your hand."

I spluttered and complained to no avail.

After three of the best he simply excused his reason by telling me." You may not be with these two but no doubt you will have been up to something that I don't know about, so we will count this in lieu."

I didn't know what the hell lieu meant but it certainly hurt. All three of us tried very hard not to look distressed or show signs of injury, at least not until we were out of the Head's office, then it was hands tucked under our- armpits and accompanied with a good amount of foot stamping. As we trundled down the corridor the pain in the other two's hands seemed to disappear for a few seconds as they realised I had got the same punishment as them but was in no way involved, a few moments of ribald remarks seemed to ease their pain but not mine.

My reason for taking so long in delivering a few papers to the heads office was accepted by Mr. Warwick, but the smile on his face was a little perverse I thought. The rest of the class joined in the mirth without a moment's hesitation and it became something I had to live with for a few weeks before the escapade was forgotten.

Once I had high-tailed it out of school at the ripe old age of 14 years, I embarked upon one of the most interesting and marvellous times of my life.

CHAPTER 7

This was to be the most exciting, or possibly the most nerve wracking day of my life. I had left home around about 7am on an old Cumberland bus, these rickety old double-deckers had no doors, which meant that although better than a bike, it was every bit as cold. I didn't even have the luxury of pedalling like blazes to keep myself warm! This was the miserable depths of January and it seemed that the cold had seeped into the fabric of the seats and could not be warmed up however much I fidgeted with nervous energy. Every stop, we stopped at every blinking bus stop, would we ever get to the station in time for me to catch the train? People on and off all talking to the conductor as he exchanged tickets for cash, shop girls chattering, full of secrets as their perfume floated by me as they headed for the top deck, market-goers hefting empty baskets and bags past everyone, it seemed like an eternity. Ding-ding the bus would stop, ding-ding we were off again. It seemed to me that everyone on the damned bus was smoking, the walls of the vehicle were a smart sort of yellow where once they had been white. I had a growing feeling of unease, but more than that, I just wanted everyone to be quiet and for the bus to get me to Carlisle as soon as possible lest I be late!

I arrived at the station about an hour or so too early (just in case) and was impatiently waiting for the next leg of my trip. Was winter as cold as I remember? It seemed that every year when I was younger, was like a Dickensian Christmas scene, hard frost and snow, winds that took the short way through the body rather than around it and a perpetual struggle to keep out the cold. I had decided to sit out on the platform rather than in the waiting room where it would have been much warmer, you never know, the train might have left without me! I breathed out the air from my lungs it was like smoke. Watching the other prospective passengers smoking on the platform I decided it would be interesting to pretend I was like the older people and exhaled rather more than I should have and started to cough - it was a rubbish game and I gave it up.

The railway station was massive, bigger even than the aircraft hangars at Kirkbride where we used to visit whenever we had nothing better to do and that could be quite often during the long summer holidays. Maybe the hangars didn't look so big because most were full of old aeroplanes and parts of old aeroplanes. We were drawn to them like moths to a lamp, what could be better for a pack of small boys on bicycles than exploring the long dead remnants of the war? We would spend hours sneaking round the sheds, in and out of plane carcasses, pretending to be a Mosquito pilot hot on the tail of some German plane or other. But, without exception every time, this infestation of small boys in shorts with blackened knees would be evicted by men in overalls who, themselves, had nothing better to do. Looking back I think we did them a favour by breaking their monotonous daily routine, I am sure they would miss us when we went back to school.

Excellent hide and seek with our pursuers as we dodged between the wheels and bits and pieces that went to make up an aeroplane and off to the perimeter fence as fast as our skinny legs would carry us. The men never really put their hearts into catching us, so we always managed the fence without being caught. Anyway we could not have carried a plane away, even between the six or seven of us it wouldn't have fit on our bikes!

A small black scruffy steam engine chugged along the far platform towing a couple of carriages brought me back to the present. That thing won't get me to Glasgow I thought and ignoring everything around it the little engine simply trundled off under the bridge and disappeared into the distance.

My attention wandered off again; I'll count the doors on the platform, they were massive compared to our doors at home, red and shiny with immaculate gloss paint, every one with a different notice in no-nonsense lettering. Ladies Waiting Room, Gentlemen's Waiting Room, Staff Only, Booking Office and so on. The Station Master's office was on the opposite platform and as I looked at the red door it was thrown open and there stood a man carrying a top hat that he brushed lovingly with the sleeve of his coat, he wore a very smart black suit and highly-polished shoes - must be the boss I thought. The game of counting the doors lasted about as long as the fake smoking.

Having asked no less than half a dozen porters where I would catch the train to Glasgow, I was still apprehensive - had I been sent to the right platform, or were each of them having a laugh at a young boy so obviously a first- time traveller? The cold bit through my clothes but I didn't really feel it - not true! I did feel it and it was all I could do to stop my teeth chattering but there was no way I was going to let on.

A porter kept popping out of a door marked STAFF ONLY and repeatedly took out his watch and made a great show of looking at the dial before returning it to his waistcoat pocket. Each time he would look across at me, gently shake his head and return to the warmth of his office, making sure the door was closed against the cold. Maybe the train wasn't coming or had it been cancelled and they had forgotten to tell me. All these thoughts raced through my head. How would I explain to the powers that be "Sorry sir but the train was cancelled?" That would never do, especially on my first ever interview.

Then it all happened, as if by magic a loud speaker burst in on my thoughts, the garbled voice informed anyone who could interpret the message, that the next train arriving on the platform was bound for Glasgow Central. I, being an unseasoned traveller, just heard the name Glasgow Central. The disembodied voice that announced the train's arrival must have had special training to garble such an important statement. To be honest though, in all the time I served on the railway I never, ever, understood any tannoy message, except the final couple of words, such as I had just listened to.

The giant Locomotive hissing steam and smoke, drawing behind it a mass of carriages, clattered obediently along the edge of the platform. Two men leaning from the cab smiling through the coal dust as the train slid to a halt, their white teeth showing through the grime. I remember vividly the shimmering heat, the smell of hot oil as this colossus seemed to stand there panting as a dog would after a good run. Red hot ashes spilled from somewhere underneath and scattered along the sleepers. A sudden eruption of white steam escaped from somewhere on top of the boiler and I almost left my skin on the seat that I had occupied a second or so ago. I felt that everyone on the station was now aware that this was my first trip on a train. Today was to be the first time for many things, not just this journey. As the two men climbed down from the engine, their places being taken by two men in clean overalls, I did not dally to see any more.

Not realising that the train would be here for at least a few minutes and, already at the edge of the platform, I scrambled at the door handle nearest me just as it opened almost breaking my fingers in the process. A man wearing a long coat and a trilby hat gave me a withering look; being me I withered him back and squeezed past him in case the train left without me. I heard a sniffle and snort something about kids, but the train would not leave without me; I was on board and looking for a seat and what's more it was warm, lovely and warm. I found a seat beside the window. Looking through the grimy glass I saw the well-dressed man in the tall hat, more marching than walking down the side of the train, gloves held in one hand rather than on his hands which I thought was very strange. He spoke to many of the passengers as he passed by and stopped to talk to the man who had almost broken my fingers on the door. Oh dear, I wonder if they are talking about me? But neither man looked my way and they walked back up the platform chatting to each other.

This journey had begun some weeks earlier while still at school. I had been eavesdropping on a conversation whilst waiting in Tom Fishers our local barbers' shop. The term "barber" was played fast and loose when describing Tom, although he looked the part with his apron, white shirt and armbands to keep his cuffs up, the man only had one haircut. Every time you sat in the chair Tom would ask you what you wanted and, regardless of your answer, would perform exactly the same cut on every customer - short. This particular day, whilst I was waiting for my scalping, the conversation I was carefully earwigging enthralled me. Both the men involved in the conversation must have worked on the railway at some time or another. They talked about early morning shifts, trains roaring past the station platform going on to far distant places. Almost immediately I could see myself as a driver on a great steam engine, guiding it skilfully single handed through valleys and mountains and on to destinations unknown! Facing the weather, the elements and countless mounted train robbers who would be foiled by my masterful driving of the iron horse! (I was a huge fan of the cowboy pictures every Saturday afternoon). What imagination!

I was fourteen years old and due to leave school in a few weeks and suddenly there it was like a flash, I knew what I was going to do. I can't remember if I got a haircut that day or not, did Tom miss out on wielding his scissors? Had I escaped the hair being partly cut, partly pulled from my scalp? Everyone I knew asked what I was going to do on leaving school and like most youngsters in those days I didn't have a clue. But now I did and I just had to tell someone. Strangely I didn't meet a soul on the way home who was remotely interested, no-one stopped to talk and when I got home, my mother being my mother, thought I was mad when I informed her of the news. "Don't be so daft, you're too scrawny for that job, big strong lads are what they are looking for." That was the wrong thing for Mam to say. She followed it up with "We will see what your dad says when he gets home, where on earth did you get that idea?" That's just what it took! I was now absolutely convinced that this was exactly what I wanted to do!

The train whistle blew, a sudden screech of steel on steel as the giant wheels bit into the rails, steam and smoke roared from the engine as it sought for traction, the couplings clattered and the great buffers groaned as the engine began to pull the train away from the platform. My stomach lurched along with the buffers; this is it I thought no going back. Did I do the right thing, was my mam right?

I thought back to the day I had the audacity to knock on the Shed master's office door, I had no idea about how you went about getting a job as an engine driver. After turning up at the station and being directed to the Shed Masters office by two sniggering men with brooms, I knocked on his door, for a moment there was silence, then more of a bark than anything I could remember as a voice said: "Come in." That was all. "Come in." So I did, I eased the large door open and peered around the edge. "Yes" The word came from the mouth of a thin, bony faced person who sat behind a rather large desk. His look reminded me a little of a bespectacled, outraged heron. "Come in and close the door, what is it you want? Can't you see I am busy?" He did not look up from what he was doing. "What?"

It was like a snarl as the words left his thin lips. He peeled off his wire rimmed glasses as he looked in my direction pen in one hand, glasses in the other.

Struck dumb by this severe apparition of a man, I had to muster all of my confidence and managed to squeak "I have come to see if I can have a job."

"I beg your pardon?" This, I would find out later, was Mr. Darcy, Shed Master whose word was law and, luckily for me, this was him in a good mood. "Well, I would like to be an engine driver" I said, gaining some confidence.

"Who in God's name said you could wander in here just as you please, you need an appointment before you see me," was his next comment. I thought this grey man in a grey suit was about to burst!

"I just thought as you are the boss, you are the person I should see and as I was told to see the Shed Master that is what I am doing." A little peevish now because of the men with the brooms who had assured me that this was the correct protocol. Oh, the innocence of youth.

His lips moved but for a moment nothing came out, I think he decided on a different tack, shaking his head he reached for the telephone that resided on one side of the desk. He barked once to whoever it was on the other end of the line. "Get in here now."

A boy not much older than me came hurtling through the door. "Yes Sir."

"Who told this youth to come and see me, was it you?"

"Absolutely not sir."

"Well take him up to the office and tell the manager to deal with it."

I was taken by the arm and ushered out of the room double quick. "How did you manage to get in there?" My guide hissed, gripping my elbow as we got outside the building.

"I want a job and I was told to see the Shed master so that is what I did."

"Well you are supposed to see the clerk first, then the manager, all very official here, you should know that before there are any more problems." The rest of what he said was lost to me as he was talking fast and more to himself than to me. His head turned and he looked over his shoulder to make sure I was in tow. There was no footpath across the railway lines, only wooden sleepers laid side by side with the steel rails running between them. Great engines moved about as if they owned the place and I supposed that being the size they were no one was about to question that fact.

We were heading for a soot covered building, I don't know why I say soot covered building because everything was covered in soot. Taking the reverse route across the same railway lines I had crossed, not that many minutes earlier, before my escapade with the shed master and pushing open the door that was just about the same colour as the rest of the building, my guide hurried inside, obviously unaware I was close behind him, the door swung to the closed position taking me by surprise. By the time I had pushed it open again, he was nowhere to be seen.

There was a corridor on my right and a staircase on my left. My impulse was to go with the corridor, however before I had taken a couple of steps his voice hollered from the top of the stairs "This way mate." At the top there was a selection of doors, one of which was marked Manager and my guide simply said "In here mate." He turned, faced into the office still holding the door and said "Mr. Darcy sent this lad over to see you." As I reached the open door he whispered, "Good luck" And hurried off back down the stairs.

"You want to be an engine driver then." The office manager inquired. He was a short, rounded man in a not too well-fitting suit, elbows and cuffs patched with leather. At first I couldn't make my mind up as to the stuff on his shoulders, whether it was dandruff or fag ash! He picked up a half-burned cigarette from a stuffed ash tray so I decided on the latter. He continued "There are however a few formalities we need to go through before we can put you in charge of a steam engine, so we will begin with your name". "George Scott sir, age fourteen, but I am fifteen in a few weeks." He never faltered, "Address? If that's ok with you?" And so, it went on.

It was obvious to me the manager knew he was talking to a budding engine driver, and I took to him straight away. By the time he had finished asking his questions my self-assuredness had begun to return "What about the uniform?" I dared to ask.

"Let's see if you get the job first shall we?" Now he had planted a little worm in my head. Maybe I wouldn't get the job, but if I didn't, it would be their loss.

All the formalities over, all the forms filled in. I was told that 'they', whoever 'they' were, would be in touch.

I thought, is that it then, nothing to show I had even been here? Nothing to show my parents? A bit of a let-down really.

Standing on the steps outside the grey soot covered building I stood and watched! The hair on the back of my neck said it all. From my position, I could look over the top of the bike shed as, one after another, great engines passed by. Some bright and shiny and cared for, some looked neglected but all of them pulsing heat and steam and power like huge steel beasts. A great rumble and a crash made me jump as a torrent of coal hurtled down a chute into the tender of one of the waiting engines. The whistle blew and the engine that had been taking on coal drew away from the coaling plant. As I watched all the goings on I began to think maybe there is more to this engine driving lark than I suspected.

"Are you waiting for something or are you lost?" The voice belonged to man in the uniform of a driver or fireman. His face was a little stern, maybe he thought I shouldn't be here. "I've just been to the office for a job as a driver." I explained. He instantly burst into laughter. "Did they give you the job then?" he said, still chuckling.

"Well not right away," was my reply. "But they are going to send for me soon."

"Good luck lad." He proffered over his shoulder as he departed across the tracks.

I had enough money for the bus fare to the bus station and my return ticket home with not a penny to spare for a bag of chips or a sausage roll. So up the cinder path I wandered.

As ever in those far-off days winter really did mean winter and truthfully even with a dozen layers of clothes on it was never enough. You had the clothes you wore and had to put up with the cold. Honestly everything was worn until you could almost see through them before they were discarded, even then they would be cut into strips to make hooky mats for the house. Standing at the bus queue was not very nice as the bitter wind found every nook and cranny plus everything that wasn't a nook or a cranny.

CHAPTER 8

It was always bitter cold in winter, 1947 was the year of the 'big' snow when I remember the white stuff being at its deepest. The banks of snow on each side of a narrow cutting were a new world to be explored for us youngsters, while for the grownups it was just another problem to deal with. The whole countryside looked the same except for the odd tree that dared to put his head above the white blanket. Looking at the cottages in Tenters they are not very big, but as a five-year-old jumping from a bedroom window into the deep, deep snow it was fun except when my Mother found out and she put a stop to it. She appeared to a little boy as a bit of a spoilsport. I don't remember the snow and cold that followed, for about six weeks after that, being a problem, but I wonder if, in these days, we would manage to cope with the weather we had back then; not only with the roads but the day-to-day necessities of life? Remember, there was no such thing as central heating and double glazing had not even been thought of.

Maybe if you were lucky there could have been lino on the floor however mainly it would be bare wood boards. Jack Frost would paint the windows every night with the most beautiful frost patterns that would be added to each night until, eventually, the patterns were as thick as the glass and that is how things stayed until the thaw. Imagine using the outside loo's in weather like that! The cistern refused to work, and the tap water needed to be unfrozen not only of a morning but many times during the day.

One dependable source of warmth was a newspaper bag of Stuart's chips from his shop in Water Street. Stuart's chips were so covered in fat (probably because of the number of times they had been in and out of the pan) they could be slipped down your throat without having to chew them first. His fish and chips were always cheaper than the other two chip shops in the town but with salt and vinegar a hungry young boy couldn't have cared less.

He had an old sandstone shed across the way, it looked like it had been used as a wash house previously and for what seemed like weeks prior to Christmas, he spent his life inside plucking chickens, ducks and geese. If you needed chips you had to go around the back of the shop and into the lane and give him a shout, he would mumble something or other and come into the shop covered in feathers. Often the fat wasn't hot enough and he would bung some dripping into the open firebox for a quick start. How both he and the shop never went up in smoke was a minor miracle.

Should Stuart be away or busy doing other things, then his rather large wife (he was small and scrawny) would launch herself (launch may be too energetic a word maybe lurch would be more suitable) into the care of the shop but often the fire was allowed to go out and rather than set to and re-light it, she would close the shop altogether or at least until Stuart returned. The vocals, as I remember, were what would now be called,, at the very least, colourful. I have a funny feeling that although it was a tough life, Stuart preferred to be in his shed plucking whatever, rather than be in the house with his darling wife.

Next door to Stuarts Fish and Chip Shop was Stoddard's Sweet Shop. It was really the front room of the house with a counter, the surface of which was covered with open boxes of sweets and on the back wall were a few pigeon holes containing packets of cigarettes such as Woodbines, Players etc. I remember every Saturday evening quite a few farm hands would enjoy an hour or so on the bench that was obviously set strategically beside the entrance. The group would discuss any gossip since they had all met the previous Saturday and put the world to rights.

Still daydreaming about hot, delicious chips I caught the bus home where I faced another barrage of questions, first from my mother, and later from dad. The interrogations always began with: "Tom are you going to tell that lad, or are you just going to sit there. You know he isn't strong; a job like this could kill him. You know he is always going down with something or another. Well tell him, go on."

Dad was more understanding about these things. "What am I going to say? you seem to have said it already." A quiet wink from dad and his head inclined towards the doorway was enough. I slipped as quietly as I could through it. As I passed his chair he whispered, "Not to worry I'll talk to your mam, when she's was in the proper mood." Another wink and nod and I was off.

Dad was a constant buffer between me and the outbursts of my well meaning, but slightly overprotective mother. My earliest memory of him was when the war must have finished, marching alongside Tenters Beck resplendent in his Army uniform with a large bag on his shoulder. He was laughing and picked me up in his arms effortlessly placing me on his other shoulder. I can't remember much else about the homecoming as everyone wanted my Dads attention; the rest of the memory like so many others has simply faded away into history.

Opposite the cottages was a very high wall and behind it was the local gas works. The retorts, massive furnaces twenty-foot-long were where the coal was cooked rather than burned turning it to gas, tar and coke. These white-hot fires were situated immediately behind the massive wall and because of the heat generated in the process of making the gas etc, the wall was warm all year round. As kids we would sit for ages on cold days with our backs up against the warm bricks. The wall had many functions; it was used for drawing on and as goalposts when we could find someone with a ball! Years later my dad went to work there, but in the early years, after the war, he managed to get a job at the Co-op delivering groceries and animal feed to the local community, and not, may I add, with a motor vehicle as the supermarkets of today do. No - this was with a horse and flat-cart and many a happy day I spent sitting in a box while he did his round. Blackie, the well trusted horse that pulled the thing for hours on end, never faltered but was well used to the stopping places for food or drink, not only for her but for the driver, (my dad) and his sidekick - me. She would pull up at the same place within a few feet of the last time she had been and dutifully start pulling at the grass on the verges, not recommended these days, but then no-one dreamt of using chemical sprays so the grass and herbs were safe for the old girl to eat. The driver and his assistant would also take advantage of these stops, the cheese sandwiches and the tea kept in a bottle supposedly to keep it warm, were something else, always that special taste brought about no doubt by the fresh country air. In summer, with all the bird songs as an accompaniment, I learned a lot from my dad in those distant days about Mother Nature but never realised at the time. Only years afterwards, things I thought I never knew would bubble to the surface and often bring a smile to my lips.

In those day's farms were more like small holdings and a lot of the deals would be on a barter system, exchanging eggs and butter and whatever for provisions such as flour, sugar, salt or other basics. With the account being settled at the end of the year or after harvest. By all accounts the farmers were pleased to see the old cart trundle down their lonning. But there was always one, as in all walks of life, and this particular one sticks in my mind. The man was complaining about the price he was getting from the Co-op for the eggs or butter. Dad tilted his head to one side and told the complainant "There's a lot of lads did not come back from the war would like to be in your shoes." And with that he clicked his tongue at Blackie and off she went. Dad looked at me and winked.

CHAPTER 9

About a year later, at least that is what it seemed like but was probably no more than a week or so, after my railway interview, a brown envelope arrived. For me! An official looking brown envelope, with my name on it! It contained a short letter of instructions and a return ticket - Carlisle to Glasgow. The instructions were as follows: you are to present yourself to Doctor Whoever, at number whatever St George Square, Glasgow, at 1pm on whatever day etc. etc. for the purpose of a medical examination and eye test. Please present this letter to the Doctor on your arrival.

Signed: Office Manager

Kingmoor Motive Power Depot.

I wonder if that was the man I met at the shed?

Smoke filled the fields as the train roared through the countryside, the carriages lurched from side to side and the wheels kept up a constant tiddle e dum, tiddle e dum. The rhythm changing only as we crossed over points, or as we hurtled through a station, tiddle e dum, tiddle e dum. I kept myself occupied with numerous visits to the toilet. I didn't want to use the toilet itself but it filled in some of the journey time and it was the only place to get a drink. I had a wander along the corridor as far as the guard's van, but got no further as the man in charge jerked his head and mouthed "Bugger off." So as a budding railway man I did as I was told and buggered off. The sudden roar of a train going in the opposite way almost pulled the windows from their frames. I never gave it a thought that this would happen a hundred times a day to every train. But it was still a shock as I was in the corridor between carriages. The one thing I was grateful for was the carriages were warm.

What I really wanted, was to tell everyone about this journey I was on, I thought they might realise that I was a budding train driver. But all the passengers were either reading newspapers or had their heads lolling about fast asleep. I thought better than to waken these people, they may not have liked it.

These passengers were still oblivious to this future train driver even as we drew into Glasgow Station. As the train stopped and people prepared to disembark, I waited to see where everyone was heading before trying to look as if this was a common every day thing for me. After all I was only a few steps from being part of all this paraphernalia that surrounded me. Everyone in a hurry, trying desperately to overtake each other along the platform, I wondered if it was like this every time a train pulled into the station. The not too distant future was to prove this to be true. The ticket collector would realise who I was, but all he said was "tickets please," in a language I could hardly understand. As I faltered for only a second "Have ye a ticket or no?" I pushed my ticket at him, I don't think he ever left his seat, he was just there. The question popped into my mind - ask him how to get to the address where I needed to be. His face said everything, purple stubby nose, tiny eyes hidden by overhanging eyebrows, I quickly moved on, he wasn't interested.

As a young boy, Glasgow felt strange. The buildings seemed to lean over into the street they were so tall. I had never seen anything to compare it with. Everyone was in a hurry, it wasn't until I managed to stop about the third or fourth person that I got grudging directions to St. George square. I had tried to ask the ticket collector but all I got was a wave of his hand and a few grunted words that were impossible to understand. Obviously trained by the same person who trained the announcer on the loudspeaker system. These passengers had places to go, places to be and I was just another obstacle in their way. Never mind, I had managed to get directions and, as luck would have it, my destination was not far from the station.

Leaving the station, the cold wind almost took my breath away, and the fine drizzle soon found its way through my shirt collar. Truly I wasn't dressed for the kind of day it was. And my coat, well, my coat was still on the peg in the porch back at home. I had pretended not to hear my mother's last command. "Take your coat or you will finish up catching your death of cold." I was a grown lad, and didn't need such a thing as a coat. Just now I could not have been more wrong. And in hindsight I wished I had not pretended to be out of earshot. Why is it that mam's are always right?

I had time on my hands, I would look for the address where I wanted to be and then have a look see what went on in the area or maybe not! However, I did notice, as I headed for the exit, the great grey pillars supporting the immense roof, the middle pillar had a commemorative stone fitted to it and beyond these a massive pair of cast iron ornate gates, and I wondered when the last time they would have been closed or cleaned. In fact I wondered if the debris wedged behind the iron railings had ever been noticed. The guy that had that job would have had to be have been a big man. And then I was outside. It was cold inside the station, but nothing like the biting wind out on the street, I needed to keep moving or suffer the consequences.

Following the directions, I had managed to get, across the road and down the first street on my right. There it was the number I was looking for. The door was twice as tall as me and the polished numbers on a large brass plate were not to be missed, even from the middle of St. George's square they were unmissable. Trying to look as if I belonged here, I climbed the few steps, turned the door knob which required both hands working together and pushed my way inside. What a relief, it was twenty degrees warmer in here and I gave a great shiver, not that I would admit to being cold or anything but that hallway, at that moment, was heaven.

A lady came down the stairs and, pausing a couple of steps from the bottom, she looked quizzically in my direction. "Can I help?" she enquired. My first reaction was to head for the door but it was warm in here so I quietly replied. "I am looking for the Doctor."

"Do you have an appointment?" She asked coming down the last of the steps.

"Yes! Yes I have." Scrabbling for the letter in my pocket, I tried to hold the crumpled envelope to my chest with one hand while trying in vain to brush the creases out with the other. Taking the excuse for an envelope, the lady turned, and as she turned she pointed to the chairs at the bottom of the stairs, "I am not sure if the doctor has gone to lunch yet, have a seat and I will find out for you." Her voice was quiet and I understood every word -better than the voice on the railway loudspeaker.

She was gone only a few minutes, but with the door not quite closed I could hear the murmur of voices in the office. The door reopened and closed quietly behind her. "Although you are early the Doctor will see you before he goes for lunch, he will call you in a couple of minutes." She informed me. With that communication delivered she disappeared back upstairs, only to return almost immediately, but now she was carrying her overcoat and as she passed me I received a half smile and a "good luck." She shrugged her arms into the coat then the outside door closed behind her.

This waiting malarkey did not sit well and in a couple of minutes I started to fidget, then rising from the chair I wandered to the bottom of the stairs, looking up wondering what was up there. A quiet voice came out of the blue taking me by surprise; I had not heard the door to the Doctors room open. "George Scott?" The question was obviously directed at me. Taken a little unaware I must have stammered a little. "YYYYes sir" I managed. "This way my lad." I was a little amazed as he held the door open and allowed me past, into what reminded me of my own Doctors surgery, smelling of medicine and tobacco. No messing about, the Doctor must have been hungry and wanted away for his lunch (another new word – to me it was known as dinner, but what did I know?) "Come over here and stand with your back against the wall". Following his instructions, I did just that. I hadn't noticed the piece of wood protruding from a stand and as I leaned against the wall he slid the wood down the stand until it rested on my head. "OK you can sit down". As I went back to the chair he wrote something in a file in front of him. "Any illness in the last few years?" he asked. I hadn't a clue so replied "None that I can remember sir." I was answering as if replying to a teacher when questioned at school. Something that would take some time to devolve myself from.

The next question although it wasn't really a question, more like an order, took me a bit by surprise. "Stand up, take your shirt off and drop your trousers."

What was all this about? the thought jumped into my head. I was more than a little embarrassed, because in those days no one that I knew ever wore underpants, and I was no exception. But I did as requested. The Doctor came around the desk, taking his stethoscope from around his neck he proceeded to listen to various parts of my back. God, that thing was cold and a brief shudder ran down my back and back up again. Then it was the turn of my chest. What he was listening for I have no idea. Finished there he placed his cold hand on my nether regions and told me to cough. To this day, I am not sure what he was looking or listening for, but I must have been OK because his next words were " Right, you can get dressed now." I had no idea how quickly I could put shirt and trousers on, I had goose bumps as big as hen's eggs but it would have been a record if I hadn't managed to fasten trouser buttons to shirt and vice versa. Never mind, the Doctor was obviously not finished.

"Stand up straight and put your toes on that mark." He pointed to a white line on the lino. "Look at the chart on the wall lad and read from the top line as far down the letters as you can." I don't remember how far down I got before he said "that's fine". He handed me what looked like a small ping pong bat. "Cover one eye and then read down as far as you can." Following his instructions again, I did just that and when I had arrived at the last letter, he said "Now cover the other eye, if you don't mind, and read down as you did before." As I arrived at the smallest letter I could read the Doctor asked me to do the same with both eyes again.

While sitting behind the door for those few moments I had looked down the eye test card and remembered it had been printed by some printers in Glasgow. As I reached the smallest letter the devil in me pretended to read the printers name. There was nothing said, he raised both eyebrows more in a question than surprise and presented me with a book. Flipping it open and still with that questioning look in his eyes he asked me to tell him what I could see on each page. At first it was a jumble of different sized coloured bubbles, "Don't look too closely." He murmured in his soft Scottish voice and almost immediately certain bubbles became numbers or letters. This was like a revelation and as I turned each page it became easier to pick out the relevant details.

"OK, that's it for now, I will be sending my findings to..." He flipped over a couple of pages of his report, as if looking for something, before saying "Kingmoor, but I can tell you that everything is as it should be. Good afternoon." Coming from behind his desk he opened the huge door and still looking questioningly in my direction he allowed me past.

All this way and for about ten minutes. I was out in the cold once again and without thinking I was heading for the railway station, still wondering why I had to cough? I thought it must be amazing to be able to tell if someone was ill just by coughing

The thin wind blew straight through me and I had to dodge what I thought must be the entire population of Glasgow, if not Scotland, and all of them going the wrong way. At least the bodies I pushed my way through kept off the main aim of that wind. And in a short time I was back at Glasgow Central. Back among the smoke and steam. This, of course, was to become an everyday part of my life.

Back to the harsh loud speaker sounds that I was still positive no one understood or cared to understand. And even more so, here in Glasgow, the voice sounded like an American auctioneer from the cinema.

Masses of people milling about, some looking for the right train, others waiting to meet relatives. Maybe some like me just wanted to be out of that withering cold wind and didn't have anywhere else to be.

Just coming into the main entrance was a Buffet (pronounced bufat by my contemporaries back home), a little unsure, I gazed through the glass door before tentatively putting my shoulder to it. Better look as if I should be here as I headed for the counter, trying to push my shoulders back as I had been taught in the Army Cadets but almost immediately, giving in to the cold, slouching back into a more comfortable position.

I had a few shillings in my pocket, but when I left home, I had been urged not to spend it unless I absolutely needed to. But it had been a long trying day and hunger is a great leveller, what I was expected to survive on for a whole day I wasn't sure. What I was sure of was that I could talk my way out of any trouble when I got back home. It would simply take a "Mam I was starving." And it would be sorted.

There were a few curly sandwiches, (which in future years I would recognise as railway sandwiches) under glass dishes, better than nothing I thought! Or maybe I should go for some chocolate out of the machine by the door. Sandwich! "Could I have one of these sandwiches please?" I asked the woman behind the counter. She was short and dumpy and what was probably a clean apron at some time earlier in its life was held in place around her middle with a thin cord. Her missing teeth and whatever it was she was eating made it difficult for me to understand "Aye, which yin?" It was a foreign language and I had to stare at her questioningly. "That yin's cheese or that yin's 'am, son." Maybe she does the announcements on the loudspeakers went through my head. "Mek yer mind up, aas other things tae dee than stan here." I was loathe to upset her and quickly said. "Better have the cheese then please." Before I could change my mind the glass bowl covering the 'food' was lifted, the aging sandwich was slapped on a plate and pushed across the counter. Eyeing me suspiciously she requested payment before I changed my mind. I very gingerly handed over funds from my small hoard of coins, she was small but maybe she could get violent! She had that trained aggressive look about her. The sandwich had a mind of its own sliding about the plate as I headed speedily for the door only to be thwarted by the waitress's voice following me like the wail of a banshee "Ye canna tek the plate oota here son." I looked at the sandwich, put one half on top of the other, turned and quickly retraced my footsteps, stepping like a cat stalking a bird in case I had to flee at a moments notice. I placed the offending plate reverentially on the counter, warily keeping an eye on the coveralled figure behind the counter. The sandwich and I again headed for the door and out on to the platform. It might have been better to stay inside the Buffet it was decidedly warmer, but I had grave doubts about the waitress and how she might react to me sitting at her nice clean table. Was she the reason the place was empty? Or was it her way of keeping the place clean without too much work on her part?

This was probably the first time in my life I had ever experienced shoddy housekeeping and stale vittles, having two grandmothers raised in the Victorian age where tea was served in a cup with a saucer, a mother who was brought up in their image and a father who was in the army who could cook, polish and mend as well as any of his female counterparts. We frequently had very little, but it was always made up fresh and by God you sat at the clean table to eat it. Dad could work miracles with a rabbit and an onion for tea.

CHAPTER 10

One of my Grandmothers, Grandmother Scott, lived near to our house in Tenters, and I am sure I was, at the very least, a pest sometimes but it was always worth a visit. I think she must have baked every day, some for herself, some for visitors (pests like me) and some for neighbours. I was always assured of a monster teacake with butter and maybe cheese. I remember the great cooking range, it took up most of one wall and was in constant use. I was told it was called a Scotch oven, and it had a kettle constantly on the boil. The kettle was so big it was filled with water from a brass tap on the side of the fireplace via a large white enamelled jug, and in turn, the big thingamy strategically placed by the side of the fire kept the water at the very least warm. The Victorians wasted nothing especially the heat they had already paid for. I can't remember this thing ever being anywhere other than on a gibbet that swung out from the side of the fireplace and directly over the flames to bring it to the boil to brew the tea.

The fireplace had an elaborate fender, it was in scale with the rest of the big oven, it even had corner seats attached at each end and brass finials along the front. Behind the fender was an array of tools like the companion set and various things to do with keeping the fire in order. I can remember chopping sticks to keep the 'Leviathan' burning and hanging around waiting for the inevitable question "What are you after?" To this I always answered "Nowt really" and was always happy to hear the reply of "You'll have to wait, I've just put that lot in!" I would sit patiently, well, maybe not so patiently.

Sitting waiting was always worth it. Sometimes I would be blessed with a threepenny bit as well as the massive teacakes.

The corner furthest away from the fireplace was taken up by a very large Grandfather clock, the slow, even, tick tock was enough to send anyone to sleep. This beautiful clock now sits in our living room and occasionally is wound up, the sound is still the same although the chimes are a little tinny now, and it still has the same effect. I wonder if, and when, my grandmother had the time to sit a while would she drift off for forty or so winks? I very much doubt it as that was never the Victorian way. And even if she did she would never admit to such a thing.

From early age I was promised that one day it would belong to me. It had been passed on to the George of the family. Unfortunately, my uncle George died at an early age and so, here it is waiting patiently for the next George in the family.

Mother Scott's house, part of which is now a block of concrete flats, had many visitors. Some of them stick in my mind, some not. One of the more frequent silhouettes in the doorway was Mary Wilson. "Just gaan up street Jane, does te want owt?"

"If ah want owt ah's capable of gaan mesel" was always the answer. The small frame of Mary Wilson would give a feint shrug and was gone; the rest of the reply lost to the departed.

"She alus caas just when I'm doin summat she'll niver larn that yin, anybody would think I was infirm or summat."

The memory I have of that little woman who lived just a few doors away, was the tale of how she looked after her Bantams. She would shuffle down the steep lane behind the Cottages to a cobbled yard two or three times a day with scraps etc. No doubt the tiny eggs they laid were useful, but in the harsh winters Mary repaid the debt of the eggs, by placing two old dining chairs back to back in front of the dying embers of the open coal fire, just a couple of feet apart, then the clothes prop would be placed from the back of the one chair to the back of other. Underneath the prop she would spread old newspapers on the floor and one by one she would bring the Bantams from the yard to enjoy the warmth for the night.

Back to my return journey, the curls on the cheese sandwich did not do anything for the taste and the time it had been under the glass put it on a footing with a piece of toast. It gave a bit of a crunch as I bit into it, the almost melted cheese allowed it to form a sort of paste in my mouth. It took more than a few minutes for me to beat it into submission but I managed it, at long last. I needed to wash the paste down and I couldn't afford a drink in the Buffet when I remembered I had seen a small drinking fountain near the entrance when I arrived and made a beeline for it.

I had to search for a few seconds or so, to fathom out how it worked, a simple push button with the word press under the bowl beckoned and on pressing it the fountain came to life as water jetted from a small tube. Maybe the water wasn't quite a jet, but I managed to get a drink. Unthinking I wiped my lips on my sleeve and as I turned away I noticed a woman sitting on a bench looking in my direction she raised her eyebrows a fraction and I smiled at her knowing what was going through her mind. Maybe she knew my Grandma?

Saved by the loudspeaker now telling anyone who would listen. Another garbled message but in the middle of that message I heard Carstairs and then, more importantly, Carlisle. Once more urgency took control and I had to get on the train. It was a different ticket collector and he gave only a cursory glance at my ticket as he punched yet another hole in it.

I tried to dodge my fellow passengers some carrying suitcases, some carrying umbrellas, almost all had newspapers wedged under one arm or the other. Even carrying all this baggage, they all jostled for position some clambering aboard at the nearest door opening and some heading towards the front of the train.

The carriages were wet and shiny, looking almost newly painted, but more likely from the cold winter rain. Steam escaped from between each of the carriages and at the front of the train, enveloped in even more steam, stood a red polished engine, poised like a greyhound waiting in the traps! Walter Mitty must have been on my shoulder as I took in the sight of that massive engine. It went through my mind I could be sitting in the driving seat of that engine and maybe in the not too distant future.

Ready to go, black smoke billowed from the funnel and from this distance I could hear someone shovelling coal into the great firebox. Would I have time to present myself to the men on the engine and let them know who I was? The slamming of the carriage doors made my mind up and I climbed on board with the same urgency I had that morning at Carlisle. For a fifteen-year-old boy who had never been anywhere further than a couple of trips to the seaside, and that was on a bus, this had been a long cold day.

There weren't many passengers on the return journey, well, not as many as there had seemed on the platform. I had the choice of seats and, with no baggage, I plonked down on a seat next to the steamed-up windows and tried to remove the condensation from the glass with my jacket sleeve so I could look out, but I was wasting my time, as a few minutes in the warm carriage found it almost impossible for me to stay awake. The last I remembered was the whistle of the guard and the train lurching into motion.

The journey home was more of a blur, I kept falling asleep and each time I woke it was with a start, hoping I hadn't missed my stop. Instead of an endless journey it seemed to take no time at all, it was only a few minutes before the train was clattering into Carlisle station. A man was standing at the doorway of the carriage and had the window down, so he could turn the handle on the outside and enable him to open the door. The draught was straight from the Baltic, and the vision of mam stood in front of me saying." I told you to take your coat."

I jumped down onto the platform I noticed the train crew climbing aboard the great red engine, after a few seconds the driver and fireman that had brought us from Scotland, alighted still chattering to the men who would take the train to its next destination. That could be me in a week or two, but I don't think the driver and fireman realised that the boy walking ahead of them was a future railway man, as I headed for the exit. And believe it or not the same announcer must have followed me from Glasgow, for the loud speaker suddenly came alive and announced "the train now standing at platform four is the..." That is all I heard as the rest of the message was indecipherable.

CHAPTER II

I am not sure if the next character I remember lived in the same house as the Stoddert's or if he lived next door. Willie Abbot, as he was known, had a small cart pulled by a small horse. I am pretty sure that Willie could have swapped places with the horse as he probably weighed about the same. The cart was a bit lopsided with Willie constantly sitting on the front corner, his feet barely inches from the ground. He made a living moving peoples bits and pieces around the town including fish for the wet fish shop. His cry to his long- suffering horse rang around the streets and was mimicked by all the kids, including me. It went something like "gid up a yard a half, gan on gid up." It was to be many years later before I learned that his name was not Willie Abbot but Willie Prince. Like many others in Wigton it was a nickname given to him, in this instance it was because when Willie was young he had slight falter in his speech, he would start a sentence with "ah, but, ah, but, ah but" before going on with what he had to say. At the back of the fish shop in a small yard, partly hidden, but not hidden well enough from a small boy, was Dracula's Hearse. Today it would be worth a fortune. A black horse drawn thing with all the paraphernalia inside, including the black plumes that fitted on all four corners of this old vehicle. It belonged to old Tom Miller, I think he got rid of it to try and get some peace from having to chase young boys out of his yard. Although covered in dust the care of the previous owner showed through, when the dust was removed with a little spit and rub with a mucky sleeve, the coachwork shone deep and lustrous. This was not the main reason for removing the film of dust, the main reason was to leave a message to the owner with regards to cleaning, rather like the motifs on white vans nowadays. The whole topside of the coach was glass with, what I recall now as, etched leaves and scroll work. No doubt someone with a better memory than mine will be able to tell me exactly.

To a young lad, Water Street was a great playground, it had everything from a fish and chip shop to hairdressers (barbers in those days) and a lemonade factory. There were at least two separate auctions, a clogger's workshop along with other small family businesses, not brought to mind (yet). I didn't realise at the time that the calves in the auction we allowed to suck our fingers were destined for the slaughterhouse; nor the baby pigs and lambs. Life was too busy for a young boy, I would take a short-cut through the auction to Church Street by wending my way through the different pens and climbing over others. It saved a vast amount of time going from one street to another providing, of course, none of the Auction Staff saw me. On reflection, it wasn't really the short-cut that was interesting, but the idea of not getting caught in the act. I don't think the staff were unkind really, but they would think nothing of bringing the obligatory Kebby (walking stick) they all carried, around my rear end -with many not caring where the weapon actually landed. Maybe that is why I learned to dance quite quickly at a later stage in my life, as sometimes it would be akin to the quick step, as I dodged the obviously fatal blows aimed in my direction.

On warm days, as well as some not so warm, old Mrs. Vickers would carry one of her kitchen chairs to the front door, sitting there for hours on end. She was happy to share the time of day with anyone passing by, wrapped in her pinney, feet clothed in old slippers - the space between slippers and pinney was a variety of varicose veins. Local gossip was the preferred topic and, as always, someone with a damaged hand at one end of the street was invariably fodder for the undertaker by the time the tale reached the other end.

Only on market day afternoons would she take body and chair indoors. Because the auction sold hundreds of black-faced sheep, drovers would let them out of their respective pens and drive them down to the station loading bays for delivery to many parts of the country. It was a sight to watch every Tuesday as those black-faced woolly animals hurtled down the street, leaping over one another and the odd passerby who was not too wary. Even Mrs Vickers could not compete with the spectacle, especially on a hot summer's day, the dust, the noise and the all-pervading smell of sheep.

CHAPTER 12

Weeks and weeks passed by, it seemed like months as it always does when waiting for news. In fact it wasn't really, it was just a few days, maybe a week or two. Is it not true you can hang around for ages and as soon as you leave the premises it happens? I had been out of the house for just a few hours doing whatever it was that boys of my age did. On returning home my dad looked up nodded towards the mantelpiece, and nonchalantly said "There's a letter for you, arrived while you were out." I am not quite sure whether there was a smile somewhere on his lips but I didn't have time to notice for sure.

I didn't so much as open the letter, I shredded the envelope in my haste to find out what it contained. The top line read British Railways, Kingmoor Motive Power Depot. My confidence left me at that moment, was it the news I wanted, or was it something I didn't want to read? For the first time that I can remember I was unsure! Should I read it? I looked at my dad for reassurance. He nodded and said, "Go on then, what does it say?" My voice seemed stuck in my throat and my hands shook.

The words came out in a torrent.

I am pleased to inform you that having passed your medical examination, you have been accepted as a cleaner and are required to present yourself at Kingmoor Motive Power Depot on the following Monday at 7.30 am. Please report to the booking office on your arrival where you will be given your instructions. Please bring this letter with you. Etc., etc.

I couldn't read the rest mainly because I had to get down to my friend's house with the news. As I left the house my dad shouted something but I pretended not to hear. I had to tell Dave, my closest friend, and hurried down the cinder path without trying to look as if I was hurrying. A few quick, short steps followed by a number of longer ones and repeated all the way to my pal's house to inform him of this amazing news. After all, not everyone I knew were on the way to becoming a driver on the steam trains, were they? He had to know.

When I arrived, what a let-down, he wasn't in. Just like the thing when you have good news you badly need to share with someone close, they are not in. His mam told me she thought he was at his grandma's. "He wants to go to the pictures and he has no money, so that is the most likely place to find him."

It didn't matter to me where he was, he should have been in when I had all this good news. Well he was not in, but I knew someone who would be, my own Grandma. That was it, without a moment to spare, I set off up the town. I just had to tell someone. My Grandma Munny was the best listener in the world, she would listen and would probably be as excited as I was.

I pulled the crumpled envelope from my pocket to show the good news to her. There was nothing inside, nothing! The letter wasn't there! I'd lost it! I pushed my hand deep inside my jacket pocket, the lining was torn so I had to reach deep. Not there, trouser pockets, not there either. I looked at my grandmother in dismay. "What will I do, I have to take the letter with me on Monday." "Don't fret lad it's not the end of the world" she said, putting a reassuring hand on my shoulder. I shrugged her hand off. "They won't let me start without the letter I know they won't."

"Don't worry" she replied, "we'll find it in time for then."

Mortified, devastated, end of the world. That's it then, I've had it. All that bother I'd been through, nearly frozen to death on those platforms, nothing to eat and some stranger saying cough while I had no clothes on.

I tried to console myself, probably wouldn't have liked it anyway. All that muck and soot, and I would have to get up early, would have to bike to Carlisle, wouldn't know anyone. I was starting to rack up as many bad points to the job as I could think of. I almost convinced myself I didn't want the job anyway.

Hands thrust deep in my pockets I retraced my steps back home, distracted by nothing, head bowed searching, searching for the missing letter. It wasn't to be found. I must have kicked every stone, every twig, every anything all the way along the road. I didn't care if mam went mad cos I'd scuffed the toes off my shoes.

Well that's it then, I kept thinking I needn't go on Monday, I know they won't let me start without the letter. I turned the key in the front door latch, it was always there! Never missing, not like my letter. As I closed the door I heard my dad's voice. "Is that you George? I think you forgot something in your hurry."

Dad was sitting there all smug with my letter in his hand. "This yours?" he enquired.

My family are not given to hugs or emotions of any kind really but, for the first time that I can remember, I wanted to hug my dad. I think he could see my mind was in turmoil. So, taking the situation in hand, he stood up, pushed the letter firmly into my hand and asked, "Want a cup of tea then?" And proceeded to fill the kettle. In those far-off days, there were no such things as tea bags just the good old Co-op 99 tea and dad has always measured the amount by eye. If there was a problem, he could be heavy handed, if not, a little less. Today had been a mini crisis. As always, a cuppa solved a lot of problems. Crisis averted he started to reminisce about when he was young, many years ago, when sixpence was a fortune and so on. He was a hard man not to love but as I said earlier, the family rarely showed emotion. Dad was really chuffed about the job, but had difficulty with any type of praise and simply said "You'll be alright."

Mam was a different kettle of fish and it was obvious she was not amused. I think she was hoping that I wouldn't pass the medical and in turn wouldn't get the job, after all I was her little lad. That said, she had spent a lot of time over this one particular offspring over the years, as had other members of my family, and wanted to be sure I was going to be alright in the future. After all, I was anything but strong! Hadn't I had just about every illness that was going, a weakling, in fact hadn't she told nearly everyone about the problems she'd had bringing me up. And she couldn't understand why my dad was so pleased. He should be taking her side and not encouraging me.

She would have to go up town and get me a new bait box. (Now called a lunch box but we never got lunch, it was dinner, only posh people had lunch.) I would need something to make tea and endless other things, overalls, boots, it would cost a fortune. Maybe deep down she was happy but never showed it. She always insisted I was not strong enough for that sort of work, maybe she thought I was doing it to spite her. But I wasn't! I just had to do it. All my life the words "you can't do that" became a spur, even today I can always be spurred on by "It won't work" or "it will never happen".

The first morning on my new job, my mam was up to make sure I had everything. Bait box, tea, sugar, a small bottle with milk in, everything in my new haversack. I thought I'd better get away before she wants to give me a hug or say something like "Don't go lad, there will be plenty other jobs." Once through the kitchen door I shouted so as everyone in the house could hear. "See yas tonight." The front door closed with a reassuring thud and I was off. Hardly a soul about for me to say "Good Morning" to and maybe let them know I was off to work on the railway, but there never is when you need to tell someone the news.

Half an hour early, I was standing freezing on the station platform, the only soul there except, that is, for the station master Stanley Wright and he kept peeping out of his office door every few minutes. He reminded me of a nosey neighbour not sure what was afoot, he was maybe related to the guy on Carlisle station that kept popping in and out of his office that morning that seemed like years ago, but in reality was only a few weeks.

There was a big four wheeled barrow on the platform near his door, piled high with newspapers, maybe he wanted to make sure no one helped themselves. I kept watching the large clock on the other platform, but the pointers hardly moved. As this thought entered my head the minute hand jerked and reduced my waiting time by almost a minute.

I was sure I could hear voices and almost at the same time I could see two heads appear, a little at a time, as the owners of the heads climbed the steps up to the platform. Both wore railway caps and it took a few seconds to recognise them. At the same time one of them must have recognised me. "Hey Scotty, is that you?" The voice echoed across the tracks, happy to be noticed I raised my hand and shouted back "Yeah."

"Where are you off to then?" Replying to his question I puffed my chest out "Kingmoor, how about you?" By now they were both crossing the bridge that joined the two platforms. "Yeah, that's where we both work, have you just started or what?"

"Start this morning" I replied. Now they were right beside me. Joe Hill slapped me on the back, "Stick with us we'll get you theere nee bother." Although both these lads were not much older they seemed to adopt a protective attitude toward me, even though they moved in different circles and, under different circumstances, would normally ignore me. Barry Wallace the second of the two lads asked. "Got any fags Scotty?" "Sorry" I replied. "Nivver mind." He remarked as he pulled a packet of Woodbines from his pocket.

"Well here's our ride." one said to the other and in the distance, I could hear the train whistle. (To this day the sound is quite evocative and still one of the loneliest sounds I know.) Hot ash, spilling from underneath the engine, lit up the area as it passed by and the screech of the brakes being applied by the driver added to, what I can only describe, as my excitement.

As if by magic the platform had filled up with passengers and as the doors to the train were thrown open, there was a surge of bodies, all trying to make sure of a seat. One of my new companions held me back, as I looked at him to see if I was out of line, he inclined his head toward the back of the train in a follow me sort of gesture, so that's what I did. We headed to the rear of the stationary train where the guardsman was standing. In his hand, he held a small signal lamp and between his teeth, he clenched a whistle. He was looking back down the train checking, making sure the porter had all the doors closed, as we got up to him he nodded. Taking his whistle from his lips but only for a second he managed "Hi lads, better get on, we're a few minutes late."

This was Special Treatment! I felt really important, first day and I was already much more than just a passenger! Very impressed I was, very impressed indeed.

The guard held up his lamp and blew his whistle. In reply the driver blew the whistle on the engine and with a cloud of steam and smoke we lurched into motion, a bit of wheel slip as we gathered speed. I remember trying hard not to fall over and look a novice in front of my new friends. I casually leaned on the wall of the guard's van as if this was not a new experience, as young people do. The conversation was carried out as loud as possible, talking without shouting and revolved around girls, drink and various other topics. If my comments were required, I found it easier just to nod or shake my head as if I comprehended everything that was being discussed. Even if most of it went right over my head I tried to join in, after all, I was now part of this organization and needed to be involved. The conversation was between the three, most of which was unheard by me, and to be honest meant little or nothing. But I had to be part of it whatever was being said.

The journey did not take long, a couple of stops to disgorge passengers on their way to work and before I knew it, the train was rolling into Carlisle station. Doors swung open and clattered back against the carriages, the Guard pushed open the baggage door and the three of us headed for what, to me, was a secret way out. Passing a ticket inspector in his little box, my new pals, having their railway uniforms on, were not questioned, but the inspector beckoned me to his box with a crooked finger. "Where are you off to then, my man?" was all he said. I had the ticket that had been sent through the post but my mind went blank, my mouth went dry and I had a job communicating with him. My new pals by now, were half way up the ramp but when they realised I had been held up for questioning as it were, came back to my assistance. "He's ok" Joe said "he is just starting today." "I don't care if he is the Queen of Sheba," the ticket inspector replied, "he can't get out of here without a bloody ticket." Then he noticed the proffered item in my hand, reached out, took a cursory look, put it in his ticket punch and squeezed the handle. Handing back my now well punched, ticket, he looked at me and sort of smiled. His parting words were "Remember ticket or uniform next time." I can tell you I never forgot that moment.

The journey from the station to the bus that would get us to the engine shed was a bit of an anti-climax. The three of us hurried through the streets to the town hall, on the way I was told "always look for a C4 bus that will get you to the shed." I still remember those few words, even though we were flat out without breaking into a run, maybe it would be undignified for young men to be seen running to work.

The town hall was a surprise, there were hundreds of people milling around, some hurrying from one bus to another. The one thing in common

- everybody was going somewhere and nothing should get in the way. The other surprise was the number of workers wearing railway uniform. And most of them waiting for the C4 bus. I felt a bit on the side-line to be honest, most of the uniformed men knew each other and greeted one another with quite ribald remarks, but all accepted with good humour, often the replies being in the same vein.

The C4 bus rolled to a stop and disgorged its passengers, who immediately dispersed in all directions. The railway men, impatient to find a seat, were pressing their way on board while the last lot of passengers had hardly got off. I don't think the conductor was very pleased as he kept saying "No need to push there's plenty of room." His words fell on deaf ears as each person squeezed into any vacant seat. Ping, Ping, the conductor rang the bell and the driver eased the bus away from the curb, I could see someone running across the town square but the driver was accelerating as if to make sure whoever he was, was not going to catch this bus. Down Scotch Street, around Hardwick Circus and on to Kingmoor, of course it managed to stop at almost every stop on the way. A flurry of activity as people left their seats to stand in the gangway as if they could not wait until the driver brought the bus to a halt. Some were alighting and having to run next to the moving vehicle in order not to fall flat on their faces. The Redfern pub, I was to get to know this watering hole very well over the next few years, but for now it was a getting off place for almost everyone on the bus, leaving only the driver, a couple of passengers and conductor on board.

The morning was freezing and dark, with very little in the way of lighting, a kissing gate allowed only one person at a time onto the shed grounds. Only the dark of the ash covered path stood out against the silvery sheen of the frost covered grass showing the way to the engine shed. More than once I heard the remark "Cold enough to freeze the balls off a brass monkey." Fags lit, streams of tobacco smoke, chatter and the odd laugh, probably at some obscene remark, followed us on our journey to the shed. The approach to the engine shed proper was cut off by rows of steel rail tracks with great engines making their way to wherever, some just finishing their journey some on their way to a job. All of this was a complete mystery to me.

The older staff seemed to take their lives in their own hands disregarding these steaming giants, they dodged each one as they headed for the booking on office. Sometimes cursed by the driver or fireman on the engine. Following my pals, I did the same thing, only without the same surety they had. I was mesmerised by these men unheeding the obvious danger they were in. The noise was incredible, steam escaping first from one side of the engine then from the other. The rasp and squeal of the wheels on the steel rails made the hairs on my new haircut stand on end, but the people around me seemed to take little, if any, notice of the constant noise.

I remember someone singing inside one of the sheds and I am sure it was the latest hit (Behind the Green Door) it seemed quite natural, as there was always someone singing or whistling, it was very much the norm.

CHAPTER 13

The new boys! There were five or six of us just standing in a group, looking at one another as if seeking guidance and wondering what we should do. One of my two new pals came around the corner and shouted "come on Scotty, you'll be late." I immediately followed and the other new boys, with nothing else to do, followed me. We were now in the booking-in area. Men with coal dust covered faces busy booking off shift, others looking at rosters, what a busy place and so early in the morning. A face at the other side of a glass partition beckoned, "Well?" was all the face said, followed by "Come on I haven't got all day." "I am a new starter." I stuttered. "Are those lads new as well?" He peeped over his spectacles "Well, Yes, I think so" I babbled. "Wait over there and take that lot with you. Somebody will be here to sort you lot out in a minute." With that he returned to whatever it was he was doing when I had so rudely interrupted him.

I am sure that us new starters were in the way amongst the jostling men as there was no pretence at courtesy. "Move" was about the nicest thing anyone said, but mainly it was prefixed or followed by a few expletives. Eventually a tall guy came out of the office waving a pipe and spilling ash everywhere. "You lot follow me." He disappeared in a cloud of St. Bruno smoke, with his new crew in tow. Into the bait cabin, God it was dismal. The lighting may have been new once, but this morning the bulbs were about as bright as a glow worm's armpit. "Right find yourselves somewhere to put your stuff." It turned out our guides name was Ernie, our leading cleaner. He was a shed labourer really and because of his habit of talking through his pipe, which was almost always clenched between his teeth, it was difficult to understand just what he was saying. But we all managed to catch his drift and each of us found places to put our mostly new bait bags, or more accurately, recycled ex- army haversacks. They stood out like sore thumbs amongst the well-used bags already on the various pegs, they were after all, the only things in the room not covered in soot and would eventually become targets for the comedians that worked there.

"Come on, come on we haven't got all day." With that he disappeared again and we all had to follow or get lost. Through another door Ernie brought us to a halt, knocked on a second door and waited a few seconds before opening it and sticking his head inside. "Are you ready for this lot?" He questioned whoever was on the other side. "Come in" the voice said and Ernie waved us all through. This office was as well-lit as the bait cabin, like a candle light and no brighter. As new starters we all stood transfixed, shuffling feet, looking at one another through the corner of our eyes not wanting to be noticed more than the next lad. "Round here boys where I can see you all" and he pointed to the other side of his desk. We all shuffled round in a more or less straight line. "Right, names?" He said and right on cue we all blurted out together each of our names. "Maybe it will be better if we have one at a time." He worked his way around each of us in turn. "Name? Date of birth?" Etc. etc. And to each in turn he said "good, good." That is, until he arrived at me, "Name? Date of birth?" It turned out I was born on the same day as one of the others. And as seniority was a big thing on the railway two people having the same birthday was not on. "Trust you to have the same birthday." he looked at Ernie, "well what now?" Ernie puffed out his chest "What time where you born" he said looking in my direction. And being truthful I said I didn't know, the same went for the other lad. "Right, both of you find out and come in here in the morning and let me know. I won't be able to allocate you each a booking on number, so you can't get overalls until then, Ok." he looked at Ernie and nodded. "Follow me lads come on." Like a little troop of soldiers, we dutifully followed our new leader, a trail of St. Bruno lingering in his wake. Out of the office under the big clock, turning right between a wall many feet high on one side and, what we found out later to be called, an engine pit on the other. It in turn was straddled by parallel polished steel rails that ran the length of the massive shed. Towering above us all were steam engines, the great driving wheels on each engine taller than the tallest in our group. As we passed each one, the heat and the smell told the story of great power, I don't know why, but that was the experience for me and I suspect for each of us as we nudged and pushed each other, still like school kids, which, until a few weeks ago is what each of us were, most only just turned fifteen. That would all change over the following weeks and months.

Part way down there was a small door set back in a recess, only a few feet from the rails, taking a key from his pocket Ernie presented it to the key hole, turned the door handle and put the lights on. They were on a par with the rest of the lighting I had seen since arriving that morning, glow worms in a bottle. The room was tiny and with the bodies pressed inside, Ernie began his spiel about what we were expected to do and what we were expected not to do. It was a long list and there was certainly more not to do than to do. Beware of moving engines, don't wander on the tracks, etc., etc. After what seemed an absolute age, we were all given a galvanised bucket each, some of which were so buckled they would barely stand up, some even had handles missing. "Right lads, we are going to the stores to get your bucket filled and some waste cotton so you can get on with the job of cleaning an engine or two."

We arrived at the stores, which turned out to be a hole in the wall with an ill-fitting window. We had obviously upset the storeman somehow, as up to that moment, he was easily the rudest man I had come across. The words he used are not for printing here. But the gist of his words implied he had never met such a load of reprobates in his entire life and, if it had been his choice, he would never have given any of the so and so bunch a job under any circumstances. It was difficult to know why he felt the way he did because I don't think he had ever met any of us before that morning.

Grudgingly he decided to issue each of us with the required cleaning oil and a handful of cotton waste. Going by the amount he allocated to each reprobate, it looked as if we were to clean one wheel each. As we collected our materials we stood in line behind our leader, who informed us, as soon as we were out of earshot of the storeman, not to worry about his remarks as we would probably hear worse when we caught him on a bad day. Truth was Ernie was right!

Each of us was allocated a job on the engine, one on each side to do the wheels, one on each side of the boiler and one each side the tender. Someone decided to inform Ernie that there were only five of us and there were six jobs. Big mistake on the offender's part, Ernie's face split into a yellow toothed grin, and he said jovially "No problem lad, you can do that after you finish your bit."

Ernie toured round and round trailing small puffs of smoke in his wake, seeing the job was done and nothing was missed. I would like to point out that the smoke and ash from Ernie's dustbin sized pipe, more than likely, caused half of the smog inside the shed. With the stem of his pipe he would point out that a bit more elbow grease would help. One wit called out to ask if he could get some of that elbow grease from the store. Ernie took it in good part mostly, but could come to the boil in a second, it was easy to see when he got riled, smoke and sparks would blow forth from his pipe, along with all kinds of swear words barely intelligible as his teeth gripped the stem of his pipe and better not described here.

Everywhere was permeated with soot, smoke and ash. Only years later did I learn that the taste left in my mouth was sulphur, the only upside was it cleared any blocked noses. Inside the shed it was always twilight, a haze left by existing fires in engines and fresh fires lit in the engines fireboxes that were just being reawakened after various repairs had been carried out. The phantom whistler was about at all times, sometimes it would be one of the fitters carrying out repairs, sometimes it would be one or other enginemen bringing their charges back to life, or more likely it would be Tabby Green doing his interpretation of Frankie Vaughan, but he was always around. I still remember the hit of the time, Green Door, with some affection as it was sung or whistled at all times day or night, but usually only the first verse.

Ernie would keep up his vigil making sure the job was done, a little chivvy here, a little puff of smoke from his pipe with a "No! No! Not like that, put some oil on the bloody cloth or it will never come clean. I am only going to show you one more time" and "I have told you before it won't work without elbow grease." By ten o clock time, we were all splattered with oil, which helped to make sure the soot and ash got really worked into our skin. I wondered what my mam would think if she could have seen her son now.

What a relief it was when Ernie called a halt to our endeavours. "Go and get your bait and I want every one of you back here in twenty minutes." Some of the better brought up lads would wash their hands. The washroom, if you could call it that, was something else! There being no plugs for the sinks was the least of our worries, a little ingenuity with the engine cleaning cotton, twisted tightly into a small bundle, would keep the water in the sink long enough to wash our hands. No soap, just a bucket with the scrap pieces left over from the hostel, God knows how old it was, and the towels! Well! They could have caused an outbreak of salmonella, if we had known what salmonella was, maybe even the plague, but we didn't know what that was either so we were safe. Maybe inadvertently all this muck and grime helped build up our resistance to these deadly bugs? Behind the sinks were the urinals. I had never seen anything like those either, I had obviously led a sheltered life. True to form all of us treated this new experience as if we came across this sort of thing on a daily basis. To say it smelled is an understatement. The actual W.Cs did have doors but none of them had locks or bolts on them. Some occupants would jamb the door with a page or two of the Daily Mirror or some such, but most of the occupants would leave the door open while they squatted, overalls around their knees reading the said newspapers. Different!

As there was no such thing as toilet paper the Mirror or whatever, was put to another use, something the newspaper was never intended for and the black print left smudges on the nether regions! This was recycling before it was ever dreamed of. I am not sure the newspaper proprietors would have been chuffed, had they known, that the railway men had wiped their ***** on their daily news.

There was a strange toilet arrangement for the whole block of cottages in Tenters. It was built on the side of the beck, you can imagine why. The other odd thing about it was, there were two holes side by side as the toilet seat, this was possibly so you could keep up to date with the neighbour's gossip whilst you went about your business. Something thing that sticks in my mind was the squares of newspaper strung together and attached to a nail behind the door. Oranges, in those days, were wrapped individually in soft tissue paper and when available, the tissue squares were straightened out and used instead of the newspaper. How posh is that? It is said that most residents of Tenters could whistle, I wonder if this was an early warning for would be users of the said toilet that there was someone already using it. How close could one get using shared facilities?

I used to catch eels in the beck, but no one would eat them, maybe that was because of where the toilets were situated, so after annoying them for a little while, they were put back to go about their business.

Tenters Beck was a little world of its own. I remember wading across to look at something in the water one day when I stepped on a broken bottle. Doc Thurlow our neighbour (in fact he wasn't actually a Doctor, it was a nickname he had been given because he worked at the Surgery) wrapped my foot in a towel and carried me up to see Doctor Goldsborough who supplied me with the first of many stitches I was to need over the following years.

Stuck somewhere in the back of my mind was an incident involving the open toilet system and a bunch of nettles. I can't, in all honesty, own up to the prank and maybe I shouldn't use the good lady's name, but it was Maggie Long. A couple of young urchins had seen Maggie dash into the toilet, obviously in a hurry. Nearby on the edge of the beck was a magnificent crop of nettles. The two boys had the brilliant idea of combining the now sitting woman and some of the nettles through the hole at the back of the facilities. It is said that the woman left the stalls quicker than a racehorse, even though her knickers were around her knees. The screams were said to be so loud that she could be heard as far away as Market Hill. The offending monster that attacked the bare buttocks was never seen or heard of from that day to this.

Remembering this incident, it brings back to mind a tale, told by my Dad, about the unfortunate woman's husband, Mix (as we would call him). Mix used to invite himself into the cabin where my Dad had his bait (packed lunch). Mix would sit down and duly open his bait box and always come forth with the same exclamation "Hell Tom, I've got cheese again!" Eventually my Dad had had enough of "Hell Tom cheese again" and shaking his head informed his work colleague "Mix, you have got to tell Maggie you want something for a change, otherwise you will have cheese sandwiches for every bait." Whereby Mix, looking very serious, replied "Can't do that Tom." Dad shook his head "Mix either shut up complaining or tell her."

"Wouldn't make any difference Tom, I put my own bait up!" And with that, he promptly bit a chunk out of his sandwich.

This same man had a good sideline in the spring months. He would finish off night-shift, cycle up to Highmoor when the daffodils were out in bloom and help himself to as many as he could carry on his bike, then off to Carlisle Market to sell them. Dad always said that only Mix could get away with such a thing without any sign he was doing anything wrong.

As we pushed our way into the bothy (Bait cabin - which I am told is something to do with Scottish slang!) the hubbub hushed a little, there was apprehension, expectation even in the air, which no one was supposed to know about. As we newcomers tried to collect our bait boxes and bags the hushed chatter slipped into silence, an air of expectancy replaced the sounds. As we each in turn tried to remove our bags from the large nails that acted as coat pegs, it was as if they were nailed to the wall. In fact, that is exactly what had happened. Some comedian or comedians had nailed the bags to the wall. The lads that had left their boxes on the benches had fared no better because the sandwiches had been taken out, the boxes nailed to the bench and the contents returned so as they looked as if they had been undisturbed.

The outcome of all this brought great roars of laughter and much cheering from the audience, with sandwiches spread all over the floor along with the lids from the boxes that flatly refused to be moved from the benches. There was absolutely no animosity! No bad intentions intended. And the only thing we new boys could do was to join in the hilarity, this was an initiation and was probably one of many to come. This was to see if we were sports or not! Every one of us was offered seats as the probable culprits moved along the benches to make room for the latest intake of possible future fun. "Come on lads sit here!" "There's room for a little one here" someone would shout.

The men in the cabin were to become part of my family and anyone game for a bit of fun and a laugh were welcomed with open arms. Sure there were one or two individuals that you learned to avoid, but by and large, the railwaymen were a happy, hardworking bunch.

"The boiler is around the corner if ye want a brew," we were informed. A couple of the lads must have been spoiled at home as they had no idea how to make tea. Maybe I was lucky, as my parents, well my dad, had always maintained that there were three things in life that everyone should learn - to swim, to ride a bike and the third was to make a good cup of tea. Many times, over the years, I have had cause to thank him for all three.

"Better get a move on, Ernie will be here in a minute!" and so the banter went on. Maybe I should allude to the swearing I have deliberately left out, but it was used in everyday language on the railway and probably in all other industry. Effin this and effin that, was merely a way of expressing the situation at the time. And depending on how much emphasis it was accompanied by, it told you instantly whether it was meant as a chide or was simply included in the conversation.

A silhouette passed by the window. That was all anyone could see as the window cleaner must have missed cleaning the glass for a couple of days, maybe a little longer. There was as much grime on the inside of each pane as there was on the outside.

The door opened complainingly! And there stood Ernie. "I can see I am going to have to watch you lot, I said twenty minutes not half a bloody day. Come on get your arses out here before the boss see's you or I will be the one that gets it in the neck. And guess who will suffer? It won't be me! Come on then move your arses down that shed." The older staff just wound him up. "Leave the lads alone, they haven't finished their tea." and so on. Being new we could not get out fast enough, after all he was the boss as far as we were concerned. Loud laughter and semi abusive words aimed at Ernie followed us from the cabin.

This job to me had been almost on a par with being a film star. But the first day seemed to be lacking something. I am sure that none of these stars had been put through what us new starters had been subject to. Between us we had cleaned what must have been a hundred-ton monster, well we had almost cleaned it! It was not yet in the new condition Ernie expected and he was about to prove to us that it could be a lot cleaner.

" Right my good lads" (These were not of course the exact words he used.) Ernie brought us to a stop beside our monster. "Who would like to tell me how clean this engine is?" He looked at no one in particular. His eyes travelled around the expectant group, each of us waiting for someone to answer. No one muttered a word. "Come on somebody must know if this is what you might call clean?" Still nothing. "Right all of you back to the stores, more oil and more waste, we will start again." There was at least one groan or maybe five in unison, as we picked up the buckets and marched off to the stores. "Mutter! Mutter, No use muttering lads we will do the job properly" and half to himself "this is going to be a long day I can see." A cloud of smoke followed him down the shed.

The oil we were using quickly turned black with the coal dust and old oil from the engine. My sleeves were already holding as much of the black stuff as they could, and as I reached up to the parts almost out of reach, gravity intervened and the oil began a slow creep down to my shoulders, meeting little resistance it was gradually absorbed into my vest and shirt, where it seemed to rest for a while, before continuing further and further down my skinny body. Not comfortable, not comfortable at all. But I was not alone, as I looked from one workmate to another, we were all in the same state. My new workmate Frank, or because of his ears, he was to become known as Loppy, came out with the crack that, if I hadn't had the same birthday as him we would have had a pair of overalls that would have absorbed some of the offending liquid. Although he did elaborate with one or two expletives mixed in. While some wise acre mentioned something about our respective parents having the same idea at the same time or words with a similar meaning.

CHAPTER 14

Lunch time! (This phrase was never used back then, it was always bait time) Found us back in the wash room, how we were expected to get the oil and muck off our hands before using the toilet was beyond me. There was no such thing as washing your hands after using the lavatory, but no one wanted to hold their tackle, as it was referred to, with our hands in the state they were in. So it was wash hands first then have a pee (I have put it in a polite way rather than use the language that was so often used in these situations).

The old gas boiler in the bait cabin was endlessly on the boil, and in constant use. I never did find out what colour it had started life, or for that matter was it ever new. Some of the fitters looked upon us as at least underlings or something nasty on the bottom of their shoe, and woe betide anyone who joined the queue at the wrong place. Sharp elbows were a good deterrent and they knew just where to place them. The fitters and the engineers looked on cleaners as something they had just stood in, and always seemed so easy to rile. They could get upset over nothing and sometimes it was difficult to know just what had upset them. Cleaners it seemed, could never do anything right, we were either in the way, not doing things right or generally a pain. It was possibly the conditions the fitters had to endure and had to put up with while they served their time as apprentices, now it seemed to be their turn to impose similar conditions on the next generation. And being total newcomers, we were in no position to argue. There was no easy ride in those days either for apprentices or for us lowly souls, and the fitters needed to keep us in our respective places, as indeed had their mentors done with them.

Everyone had their own mugs for tea and some of them had been without a wash so long; tea could have been made without the use of tea leaves in some of them they were so brown! There was no such thing as tea bags or coffee for that matter. The only thing that resembled coffee was in a bottle, a treacle like substance called Camp. Tea was normally already mixed with sugar in a jar or a tin, whereas some people had small oval tins with a lid on each end, one end would contain tea while the other end held the sugar, I was one of the latter as my mam thought this was the proper way!

The contents of the bait box could be anything, anything cheap that is, most often in mine would be a tea cake with cheese or maybe meat paste. But the teacakes were something to get your teeth into. Tilly Studholmes tea cakes were the best and together with co-op cheese, made great bait - at least for the first few days. I learned never to ask if there could be anything different. The stock answer was "When you earn a wage packet then you can look for something other than cheese." But mam gave in and after that I had a choice of meat paste, corned beef or of course... cheese! Sometimes Co-op cream crackers to go with (you guessed it!) cheese.

Cheese in our house was one of the few things, amongst tea and bread and butter, in ready supply. There was always a pot of tea on the stove, in various stages of stewed, and usually a loaf to hack bits off and smear with butter (my slices were always 2" thick at one end and tapered away to nothing at the other, much to the disgust of Mam, my favourite bit was the crust and I once caught hell for cutting off both ends of the loaf to make a buttie!) The cheese was always the best available as my Dad, once he came out of the army, got a job with the local Co-op. Amongst his duties, which involved delivering groceries with Blackie the shire horse and cart, collecting eggs and dairy from local farms, he was in charge of the cheeses... The Co-op had an enormous cellar, boarded out with plank shelves and festooned with ripening cheeses, all of which had to be turned and tested by my Dad with the special cheese key that hung behind the door. Every so often the cheeses had to be sampled, and funnily enough, the best, saltiest and tastiest ones always seemed to end up at our house.

My Dad worked at the Co-op after the war. His first job on a Monday morning was to turn the cheeses in the cellar. As he turned each one and, depending on its age, he would use a key that looked rather like a water tap which he would push into a cheese, twist and pull out a small sample rather like a cork from a bottle. After inspecting the exposed end, he would then smell it and taste it. I spent quite a bit of time then with my Dad and testing the cheeses was one of these treats (perks of the job they are called now). If he came across a particularly good cheese he would send me up to the shop floor to tell the rest of the staff. Not all the good cheese was sold! It seemed that the same would happen to the good hams and the bacon. To this day I have not lost my love of cheese or bacon or ham.

One time there was a great discussion amongst the staff about a new phenomenon and to a single person, they were in complete agreement that this new innovation was destined for the scrap yard from the start. Everyone has heard about sliced bread! Haven't they? "It'll niver catch on. It'll niver catch on in a month of Sundays." That was the talking point for weeks apparently, and the customers all agreed.

The deliveries from the Co-op were done by horse and cart. This was part of my Dads job. He seemed to know everyone and would be happy to pass the time of day with all he met. The groceries were packed in specially made wooden boxes, everything was either in brown paper bags or in the case of butter, bacon and such, wrapped in greaseproof paper. All these items would be disgorged onto the customers table along with the daily chit chat. Often, when out in the country, these groceries would be exchanged with eggs, butter etc as part payment. There would be the odd egg or so for Dad as a thank you, so the family never went hungry.

The boss of the Co-op was a friend of my dad so when eggs arrived, and the local shows were on, they would sort out a dozen or so, ones that matched and were the same colour etc, and present them in the show tent. I don't know how many prizes they won between them - I do think there may have been more than a little suspicion amongst the judges, maybe someone in the know tipped them off, but they decided to quit while they were ahead.

The local shows were a main event back then, some being Village shows and some that commanded a visit from all and sundry. Most of them being the highlight of the year and great pride was taken in the outcome and number of people exhibiting. Everything from home-made cakes, flowers, and vegetables of every description, horses, cattle, and sheep you name it, if it could be judged it would be included in the show. One thing always managed to draw remarks from the crowds was walking stick carving. It was incredible to see what was possible with patience and skill.

Cumberland and Westmorland wrestling was always a great crowd pleaser, along with catching a greasy pig or climbing a greasy pole. One well known person, always an exhibitor, was barred from showing his rhubarb at any of the local shows, as it was alleged that he had used a piece of wire in each stalk in an effort to keep it straight and to add a little weight to it. How true that was I am not sure, but in all future shows the offending sticks were cut in two by the judges.

Even so, I often thought that a growing lad could probably live on more than just cheese alone!

There were times when bait time could be traumatic, as we were never sure where we could sit without upsetting anyone as the fitters had to sit in their place, the words often heard were. "Come on move, that's my bloody seat you young ***** **** you're not at home now". A few other choice words were almost always mixed in for effect. As soon as the fitters had eaten, one or other of them would get out the fives and threes board. I had never heard of this game but it was by and large their chosen game, it involved much crashing of dominoes on the surface of the table, and pins moved along the board to coincide with the number scored with each domino laid down. Not for me though, or any of the new boys, it was time to do a bit of exploring.

With craned necks and looks of awe, we set off around the shed before Ernie came to look for us. Each engine seemed to be bigger than the last, each with its own number written in gold letters, many under steam (one of the many terms we would learn as we progressed over the weeks and months to come.) Steam raisers would clamber off one engine and onto the next, and to be honest, we did try to keep out of the way, but it never seemed to work, whichever way we chose we were still in someone's way. It was possibly at this time that we learned the proper railway language. For instance, "not that effin way! this effin way!" and so on. We were soon to learn just where to place the expletives. To any of the new boys, steam raising was a simple matter of throwing a few bits of wood in the opening of the fire hole putting a match to it and covering the burning wood with coal. We were to be proved totally wrong and as the months passed most of us would learn the hard way.

"Alright where the hell are you?" It was Ernie on the trail of his missing crew. In the coming months we would slip quietly under an engine or coal waggon and not let on where we were, but for now the new boys came quietly.

CHAPTER 15

Finishing time - no bells, no whistles, no hooters to tell all and sundry as all the staff, finishing at that particular time, were already at the booking office ready to go. A bit of a jostle here and a little push there but not at all aggressive, more like in a queue for the cinema with an added bit of banter.

It had to happen, both Loppy and I were held back because we did not have a booking on/off number and until everyone else had booked off we had to stand and twiddle our fingers. "Right you two you can go but don't forget you need to find out what time you were born otherwise you will need to stay until last again tomorrow."

Maybe it was meant to happen, as I left the office I bumped into a fireman who hailed from my home town, "Where are you off to Scotty?" he asked.

"I'm going to catch the train home."

"Hang on" he said, "I'll be back in a minute."

"I'll miss the train" I replied feeling all agitated, my pals had already left, they weren't for waiting for me as they might have missed their transport home.

"No you won't, hang on there." He was called Ian. He leaned through the booking office window and exchanged a few words with the clerk. Turning in my direction, he called "Come on with me." I was a little bit more agitated by now, I was obviously going to miss my train home but being a young lad, and my first day hadn't yet removed my school day thoughts of obeying the older person, I did as I was requested and followed him.

Outside now, Ian climbed up onto the footplate of a large black steam engine, beckoning me to follow him. Me! On the footplate of this great engine! I could not believe my luck. Tentatively I climbed up the steps to the footplate. So excited, at first my feet couldn't find the steps, then my bait bag got tangled in the hand rails, trying not to look flustered was difficult, but I tried. Ian, my new-found friend, simply grabbed me by my jacket and effortlessly plonked me in the middle of the footplate. There, on a seat was the driver right next to where I was unceremoniously plonked. I wasn't sure what to do, was I supposed to be here? Was he going to tell me to get off? Maybe even play hell with Ian for allowing me on board? No, in fact he welcomed me, well more or less. "This the first time on an engine then?" All I could do was nod. "Lost your tongue?"

I simply blurted out "it's hot on here." Both men laughed. "We are going down to the station, want a lift?" Want a lift? Of course I wanted a bloody lift! Who wouldn't want a lift on a real live steam engine, and on the main line. "If that's ok?" I managed to squeak."

I was told I had better sit down. Ian pointed to his seat opposite the driver. After rotating a large wheel on the tender, the driver smiled more to himself than to me or Ian. Lifting a large lever, the engine released a cloud of steam and gently we started to move.

I couldn't contain myself, the smile on the inside reached my lips and stayed there while the two men laughed out loud. I can't explain the feeling, not in words anyway, the smile on my face said it all. A kid with a huge toy. The great black engine creaked and groaned as it got under way, after a couple of minutes rocking and rolling we were over the points, past the old shed that housed the steam crane and were approaching what looked like a big hole in the ground, it was difficult to see in the winter darkness just with the glare from the firebox. This turned out to be the turntable, engines needed to go in different directions at different times and it is best to have them facing the right way on the train.

Today the engine was already facing the right way and we bypassed the table. With a screech from the metal brake shoes on the great driving wheels, the engine came to a halt. Ian climbed down the steps and headed for a small box on a telegraph pole and lifted out a phone, after a few seconds speaking to someone he replaced it and headed back to the engine.

After a couple of minutes the driver said "that's it we are off," letting go of the brake and with both hands he lifted the regulator, with a great hiss of steam the engine slid into motion – we were off. Wheels screeching, steel against steel, we joined the main line to Carlisle station, a couple of short blasts on the whistle to acknowledge the signalman, we were on our way.

It was like riding on a monster dragon, the steam, the smoke and the white heat from the fire. Goods trains passed by clattering and whistling, as if in recognition of fellow railwaymen, in turn the driver would whistle back. How was this? I thought, first day at work not even a uniform and here I was on the main line, on my way to the station. Maybe I would wake up in a minute or two and find it was all a dream. The engine picked up speed, it was almost impossible to talk, what with the sounds from the steam exhausting from the chimney, the clatter of steel wheels on steel rails, the beat changing as we crossed a series of points, and everything said between driver and fireman had to be done in a raised voice.

Rocking from side to side this was an experience of a life time, probably never to be equalled, Ian fed a few shovels of coal into the firebox, for a moment I thought maybe he would give me a go, but he closed the door on the fire hole and we were in almost darkness, apart from a flickering light from a small lamp hanging next to the sight glass on the injector.

The lights from the station showed in the distance and as the distance got less the lights got brighter until we were pulling onto the platform. It is always the same as soon as you are enjoying something it comes to an end, and it was time for me to depart from the greatest adventure. The driver slowed the engine almost to a stop but not quite "Get going or you will miss your train." Showing off a little as I stepped or rather jumped the couple of feet or so, I tried to make out this was a normal thing for a young lad to do and instead of looking where I was going, I almost ran into a baggage barrow. Even though I may have looked a bit of a twit, nothing could subdue the feeling inside, I stood about ten feet tall and it was not until I was sure the engine was out of sight, that I broke into a run so as not to miss the train home. In my mind it didn't seem the right thing for a budding engine driver to be seen in a hurry

It was obvious, I was the first person ever to ride on a steam engine, after getting off the footplate and on the train that would take me home I couldn't wait to tell my pals. But they just laughed, they were old hands and informed me that if the right driver was on duty up to half a dozen of us could scrounge a lift. Whatever they said, they could not subdue my feelings, my excitement, my first day at work. Black as coal dust and as happy as a pig in whatsitsname.

The train was leaving the station and I, with my two new pals went down the slope from the platform. Ex-army rucksack on each of our shoulders, laughing and joking, pushing and shoving one another, as we headed for home, each with his own notion of what they would be doing after tea.

No one had a chance to speak during tea time, the information about my day took all the conversation which, of course, had to include my ride to the station on a steam engine. All of it took precedence over what anyone else wanted to say, my voice bulldozed its way through whatever. So everyone decided it would be easier just to listen. My mam and dad simply smiled, after all this was obviously the first time anyone had ever had a job, so it was important for them to listen.

Fifteen years old just started my first real job I was of course old enough to shave or so I thought. I had considered this for many weeks, but how to start? My dad used a razor that had to be taken to pieces to insert the blade and I was no engineer. However, my oldest brother not long back from the army had some of the latest razors in a box, that's the thing, he will never miss one. Saturday, after teatime, seemed as good a time as any for this. My brother, Norman, had already left the house for destinations unknown. Older sister Mary was busy making sure she looked good for going dancing. My parents and my other siblings would be watching the still new-fangled television, I would be going out with my mates. To my knowledge not one of them had started to shave so it would be one up for me.

It seemed to be a requirement to soak my face with hot water, now for the shaving brush I sloshed it about in the hot water and proceeded to lather it with the bar of shaving soap, now to transfer the foam to my chin etc. My face dutifully lathered my first problem was the mirror it kept on misting over with the steam from the hot water in the sink, it was almost impossible to see which part of my face I was to concentrate on first. A wipe over with the damp face cloth seemed to solve the initial problem. Now it would be easy, hadn't I watched my dad a hundred times. Placing the razor to my cheek rather tentatively, I began. The first couple of strokes easy, then my top lip got in the way and I almost jumped out of my skin as the unforgiving blade bit into the skin and blood welled beneath the shaving lather. Before I could do anything, the white lather first turned pink and then crimson. What am I going to do? I grabbed the towel from the side of the bath to try and stem the blood. Hell I was going to bleed to death! Then I remembered the aftershave, that would do! Still holding the towel to my lip, I pulled open the cupboard door there, Old Spice. Pulling the stopper from the bottle I liberally splashed some of the contents in my hand and applied it to the laceration. "Bloody hell!" I remember distinctly following the bloody hell with my own version of an American Indian war dance.

Dads' voice resonated up the stairs. "Are you alright?" was the question. I didn't want him coming up and finding me covered in blood and shaving soap. "I am alright Dad, I just dropped something."

"Dropped something? It sounded like a herd of bloody Camels, get yourself down here Dai is waiting for you. You take more getting ready than some lassies."

"Won't be a minute."

"Hurry up the lad is sick of waiting."

The second day at work was almost a duplicate of day one. Except Loppy and I had to check in with the office about our time of birth. It turned out that Loppy was about four hours older than me, so he took preference for seniority, his clock number 588, mine 589, so from then on any job that came along, he had first choice.

Now we were entitled to overalls, and were duly dispatched to see Mackie, I never got to know his real name, he was just Mackie. To us youngsters and I suspect to a lot of older men at the shed, he was almost like the shed master. He looked after the supply stores and he allocated labouring jobs, such as shed sweeping, cleaning at the hostel, emptying wagons full of sand or coke for the boilers and all the paraphernalia that went to keep the shed running. All and sundry kept on the right side of this man, not only could we earn double or more wages if he handed you a labouring job, but he was the keeper of the stores and he could decide if you really did need a new coat, new cap or a job labouring.

Knock and wait, it said on the door, that's just what we did. "Come in." it sounded more of a command than a request, but we did as we were asked. "What do you two want?"

"We have been sent to get overalls." we were still standing by the door.

"Close that bloody door and come over here don't let all the heat out." In the middle of the room there stood a large potbellied stove, his desk obviously placed strategically beside it. It was so hot some of the stove was glowing red.

The store smelled of old sacks and soap, and it reminded me of the smell from my grandmother's cellar, but it was as warm as toast.

"Do you know what size overalls you need?"

" No sir." it was back to school again as we both answered.

"Stand up straight." Mackie growled rising from his desk. We had some way, or another upset this man but could not work out how.

"You look as if you take a small" he said without looking at either of us. He took overalls and a couple of serge jackets from a shelf and handed them to Loppy who happened to be nearest and in the blink of an eye, did like- wise for me.

To this day I still think we had to take pot luck. And to prove a point, the following morning arriving at work Loppy's trousers were trailing on the ground while mine were at half- mast. Likewise, the sleeves on Loppy covered his whole hands while mine were half way up my arms.

The main item of apparel was the railway cap, this was more than just the badge that adorned it, the hat marked the wearer as a railwayman. This could have been a big let-down, as try as we might the caps either sat like a pea on a drum, or unceremoniously slid down obscuring our eyes. After going through the whole process again and again Mackie lost patience and growled "Take one each and bugger off! Make the bloody things fit, or come back in a month or two when the new stock comes in."

A cap was a cap and the main item. So not to upset Mackie, we each took the nearest to fitting and left.

"And don't bloody well hurry back." Followed us through the closing door. During the seemingly endless process, this was akin to Jack Sprat, as it occurred to each of us that maybe we should exchange at least the trouser parts, maybe that might help? Even though they had the tags on with the same size numbers the trouser swap worked out great, the jackets would just have to do. The caps? They were something else, it wasn't until someone showed us how to fold pieces of newspapers into strips and push them under the leather brim inside the cap band that we eventually managed to stop them slipping down over our ears and eyes.

Thankfully, we were required to provide our own boots, otherwise, due to the railways "one size doesn't fit anybody" policy, we may never have been able to walk again.

Boots and shoes were always a bone of contention when I was little. My Mother always seemed to be on the warpath. "Money doesn't grow on trees, you will have to take them up to Polly Bowman's and get them heeled, soled, or whatever's needed." Polly Bowman's was an unusual set up. When they were on business i.e. shoe or clog repairs, the entrance was through the front parlour. The front parlour had a table in the centre with a large plant in the middle of it, seats against one wall and crates of lemonade down the other. I don't know how Polly ever made a profit, once she had taken the offending footwear, invariably she asked if she would put the cost of a bottle of pop on the price of the repair. She always said it would be alright. No one would see Polly again until either some other customer called or the offending footwear was returned. In the meantime, the number of bottles in the crates by the wall diminished sometimes at an alarming rate. From time to time the old lady would pop her head around the door frame and ask the same question "have you not finished that bottle yet?" I am sure she knew that it wasn't the same bottle and maybe she would add a few coppers on to the repair, but never said anything. She must have wondered why there were always a few boys even though there was only one lot of footwear to be repaired.

Sometimes when going down the backway as it was called I could hear Polly's husband working away on his last, fixing shoes. However, a lot of his work would involve repairing clogs, stitching the worn uppers, or replacing the wooden soles. But mostly it would be removing the worn-out metal corkers. After being abused by the wearers seeing who could make the best sparks kicking the corkers along the pavement.

Mostly he was an amicable man and I could sit and watch him cutting leather to shape or tearing the old sole or heel from a shoe. An old wooden box held all the tacks and nails for his work and an old jar full of black substance held a brush that was liberally applied to the repair, a quick polish and another job done. A thing I do remember, was he always kept the shoe nails in his mouth and he always hit the sole of the shoe before he hit the nail. I wonder how many nails he managed to swallow. If he wasn't in a good mood I knew instantly it would be wise to disappear as he always said, "What dis ta want? Nowt? Well bugger off then."

Arnison's of Wigton, Silloth and Penrith, as was stamped on their bottles, made the best lemonade in the world even better than the Co-op, especially if you were thirsty. The bottling plant was situated at the top of Water St. In summer when it was in full swing, the rattle of the lemonade bottles could be heard from far down the street opposite what was a group of buildings in various states of collapse called Vinegar Hill. (This must have been the local term for the dilapidated buildings I am sure, but am unaware how it got the name, maybe because vinegar was distilled here or at least bottled.)

The voices of the men working inside the buildings stick in my mind as if it only happened yesterday. The sound of the rattle of the lemonade bottles clattering around the old conveyor and the plumes of steam from the washer where the empty bottles were taken from the crates then placed upside down to be washed, are all vivid in my memory. The workers all wore rubber aprons and wellies as the place was always awash with water. The owner seemed to do all the mixing of ingredients, as if it were some secret recipe that needed to be kept from everyone including the workers, one especially was the recipe for Vimto. Now I think it was just cordial mixed with water, but in those far off days we believed it to be a big secret.

I remember the old rounded stones placed at the base of the door pillars put there to stop the old cart wheels from damaging the sandstone uprights. These stones were put to good use by the more senior of the workers as seats. They would be used during their breaks from the endless clamour of the glass bottles inside. It always seemed to me to be the perfect job and if I was rich I could get a bottle right off the production line for a couple of pennies. If I didn't have any finances, which was more often than not, then I would scrape old labels off a few crates of empty bottles which would earn me a bottle of Vimto or Dandelion & Burdock.

CHAPTER 16

After the second day shift I was half expecting to get a lift on the engine going to the station, but it was a different driver and I had to go with the lads on the bus. If my bike had been up to cycling from the station to the shed, I would have brought it on the train and saved bus money! I would try and bring it up with my parents that it would be a good idea to get new parts and tyres and thereby save some money.

My bike was a loosely bolted together collection of miscellaneous parts salvaged from the local tip, swapped from other old bikes and had tyres like sausage skins. On more than one occasion I had to stuff the ever puncturing tyres with grass from the verge, just to get me home from whatever foray into the unknown I had been on. Probably not the most reliable vehicle on which to get to work.

It was a day or two before the right moment arrived and when I did eventually broach the subject, my dad thought it was a good idea. But rather than getting parts for the one I already had, he knew someone at work who was selling a good bike, but he wanted ten bob for it. He said he would ask if it was still available next day.

The ten bob was the problem.

I was in for a surprise on pay day, so were my new pals. As we stood in line for our weeks' pay packet, the older guys in the queue informed us that we would not get paid that day as we had to have a week laying on. "What's a week laying on then?" I asked the man standing next to me. Smiling he informed me that the office could not do the rosters in the same week as we worked. Not one of us realised we had to have a week's wages laying on.

What a blow. I had spent the last few days deciding how to spend my wages. And now there was to be no bloody wages until next Friday. What about the bike I had set my heart on? What if the guy that owned it wouldn't wait until next week? I was in a fair old state when I got home, all the plans I had made for the weeks to come were in tatters.

Dad laughed, "Its nowt to laugh at." I said sharply, "what if the man won't wait till next week?"

"Have a look out the back door," he said with a great big smile.

It was there! The bike was there! Leaning against the wall. Dark green and, to me, as good as new,

" It has gears" I almost shouted, I needn't have done, because my dad was right behind me.

" Now listen," he said looking me right in the eye, "you will have to pay your mam as soon as you get your pay next week. Whatever you do, don't let me down." He tilted his head to one side, which he did when you knew he meant it.

"Dad it will be the first thing I do next Friday, I promise." He reached out to ruffle my hair, but I dodged his hand. I was too old for that sort of thing. He smiled and went back in the kitchen while I got to know my new friend.

The first trip on this new bike (well, new to me) was brilliant, though not as memorable as the first run on my first bike, my bitsa, that velocipede was a work of art that would have shamed any of Tracy Emmin's attempts at art.

You must understand that my forays to the tip were not long after the end of WW2. This was an era where absolutely nothing of any use or value would have been thrown away. Everything was reused, re-purposed and re-made, which will go a long way to explaining why my first bike had two different wheels - two different sized wheels I might add - and a seat rescued from a burnt rubbish heap. It was just possible to make out it was, in fact, a bike seat. The chain came from the same source, no mudguards and the only brake power was when I placed the sole of my shoe on the front wheel. One of the pedals was longer than the other, this made me look as if I had a limp as I peddled along. I was proud of that machine. Indeed, I took the trouble of hiding it each time I went on the ratch for other parts to help finish it off. I didn't realise it at the time, but finishing it was never going to happen, and sooner than I thought.

It was time to take it on the road, first time away from where it was built – our local tip, the source of all the parts – it had been designed and built on a "just in time framework". i.e. I found the seat just in time and the wheels just in time and so on. I wheeled the machine to the track that led down to the road. And lurched it into motion, I say lurched, as that is exactly how it happened, no thought given as to how I would successfully bring it to a halt, should need be, only the excitement of seeing how fast I could go.

This was not something I would advise now, but to a youngster who had just built a bike from scrap parts, this was at least a great adventure. I was rolling now, no time to think about consequences or any of that crap, this duo was heading for the road and it seemed nothing was going to stop us. Question – What if the ash car was coming up the hill at the same time as we were heading in the other direction? It never entered the head of this lad, he was too intent on making sure the wheels stayed on, at the same time he was trying to keep his bum on half a seat. I had never been so excited or so scared. Now was the time to apply the brake (in this case the sole of my shoe.) It made not the slightest difference, the bike was going like stink and the sole of a shoe was not going to work, maybe it was a problem with the design? I was approaching the tip gates and my luck was in, they were open. Now I had a choice, either head for the hedge on the other side of the road or try and steer around the corner. We two could make it and I decided to turn right. A bad choice as it happens, don't get me wrong, we made the corner alright, but met up with yet another unforeseen obstacle.

He had been to feed his chickens, and just happened to have a cloth bag full of eggs. The look of amazement on his face needed to be seen to be believed as he tried to throw his hands in the air to protect himself, but he had forgotten about the eggs. I don't think I hit him, but I did hit the eggs. The bike along with its passenger cartwheeled passed him, collected the handles of his bag and projected them into the air at great speed. I can see them to this day as each egg left the bag and in slow motion cascaded through the air. Each egg made a sort of thwacking sound as gravity brought each one to rest in the grass verge.

"You bloody idiot! You young bloody idiot, where the hell did you come from, have you no thought for others gallivanting about in that way, you could kill someone." I wasn't listening as I tried to extricate body from machine. Somehow the bike wanted to keep hold of the body that had been instrumental in the collision, and at first tried very hard to keep a hold of the instigator. After another volley of abuse from Mr. Little, which gave me an extra spurt of fear, the bike and myself were free of one another. I was on my feet before Mr. Little, and maybe a good job, as I am sure there was to be, at the very least, a beating if not a death in the offing. A single finger caught my sock and for a second I thought he had me, but the socks were old and after stretching somewhat, gave way and I was free and off like a stone from a slingshot.

Here was that famed local saying, following my escape from Mr. little. "I know who you are! Wait just you wait till I see your dad, you will be in for it, you haven't heard the last of this you bloody hooligan."

Better not go straight home if he knows who I am. I took the second turn that lead to the back of our house, up the old cinder path. Better wait and see if he turned up at my door. I decided to call on my pal Dave, that would take up a little time and I could see if Mr. Little would follow up on his promises.

After what seemed a long enough period for Mr Little to cool off and of course no mention of the little mishap to family, I decided to venture back to the scene and salvage what I could of my bike. Apprehension was too mild a word for my feelings as I stole along the road to the collision site. Gone! My new-found mode of transport was gone. I was sure this was definitely the place, maybe I had left too long a gap in going back. Something made me look up, maybe it was a shadow, I don't remember, but there was Mr Little not five yards from me. The massive smirk on his face told me I should not have returned, he had obviously been waiting by the gate to see if his tormentor would return and I did. "You won't get away a second time you little bugger," were his first words, I didn't wait to hear his second. I left the possible death scene without a moment's hesitation, feet slipping on the grass in my haste. There was no way this hulk of a man was going to lay a finger on yours truly. He hadn't quite timed his lurch to perfection, the only thing he managed to get hold of was the heel of my shoe, but that didn't stop me as I left him, once again prostrate, nursing one of his fingers that had managed to connect. Home was the best place for this young hooligan and that was where I headed. Not a word left my lips about the incident, and it had passed into history before I heard any more about it. My dad brought the subject up a few weeks later when he said to my Mam "Old Mr Little was asking me if any of our boys had lost a bike, but he seemed ok when I told him none of the lads had a bike. He told me the bike was in his shed if I heard of any one losing one." With that my dad looked at me with his head tilted to one side, as he did!

CHAPTER 17

The second week at work followed much the same pattern as the first, only this week I had my overalls and my new railway cap on, which made all the difference to me. I proudly clambered aboard the train to work and took delight in walking straight past the ticket collector at the gate on Carlisle station, he simply smiled and waved me through - I was part of the organization now, what about that?

Friday was different though, as we gang of five newcomers waited in the queue for our pay, along with a lot of pushing and fidgeting. I think it was the excitement of our first pay packet. We were all told we were required to join the union. Not, "would we like to join the union?" more a case of "you will join the union, make sure you see the official." Sure as shot, the union official was waiting at the pay office to make sure everyone "tipped up" as they say. He was a large guy by any standards. About three or four times my weight, but nothing like the broad-backed railway men who spent their lives shovelling coal, much more like an overfed fowl being fattened for Christmas, bursting out of a uniform that had once fit a considerably smaller man. He had a face like a slapped arse, as my Dad would say, and he was smugly standing there with his little note book in his pudgy hand ticking off names as they paid him their subs, as they were referred to. The other hand, palm-up, held out to receive the cash.

Until this day, one way to raise my hackles is to tell me I must do something, not the right approach I am afraid and as he held his hand out for the statutory shilling I simply shook his hand, collected my pay through the window and walked on. He blustered and snorted, all fifteen of his jowls jiggling at once, hurling a fusillade of abuse. He made a good attempt at trying to involve everyone around him. "Did you see that? Still has the nappy marks on his arse, I'll have to keep an eye on that cheeky little sod" That was Mr. Hughie Styler. What upset him most of all was the rest of the gang followed suit, and the rest of the men in the queue couldn't help laughing. I can honestly say I never managed to see the man do anything, he was always busy on union work, but fair to say whenever I set eyes on him or him on me he had a fearsome glower. I do think to this day I had thoroughly upset the man and luckily, we never had to work together.

One of my previous encounters with a fat man in a uniform was when my older brother, who was in the Border Regiment Cadets, would not let me use his greatcoat that had been issued to him as part of his uniform. Not only did he wear the thing, but on cold winter nights he would put it on his bed, rather like a modern duvet, only this thing was a ton weight and would keep you warm on the coldest of nights. OK, I thought, if he won't share I will join the Cadets and get my own greatcoat. On the next night for the Cadet's assembly I persuaded my brother to take me as a possible recruit and, unaware of my motives, he was happy to do so.

Mr. Carrick, a local decorator, was the Captain Mainwaring of the day and I was welcomed to the unit. "Just what we need, young blood." Well young blood was the last thing I intended to give, but you never knew what the price of an army greatcoat would be.

To be honest, the time I spent with the group was really interesting. We were taken all over the county, including the castle at Carlisle where we mingled with the grown men from the T/A, and of course we met the real soldiers from the Border Regiment. They were great at showing us what we shouldn't be involved with. Like my first whiff at a Woodbine or a half of bitter in the T/A mess. (Mam was told it was Bulmer's cider when asked about the smell on my breath.) The ex-soldiers thought it was amusing to watch, as we inexperienced kids just about coughed up our lungs with the smoke from the Woodbines or threw up our suppers with the effects of the bitter. I don't smoke now but still enjoy a glass of bitter.

These T/A soldiers would think nothing of allowing any of us cadets on the rifle range with live ammunition or go on parade with, what was after all, one of the most lethal rifles of the time - the Lee Enfield 303. We would be told of endless stories of this weapon. I am happy to say I was never required to use one outside of the range. From time to time we were all taken on manoeuvres. The T/A always in charge and always on the lookout for lads that showed promise as possible soldiers. Some of them did go on to join the army and did do well including my elder brother. But it wasn't for me.

As part of British Rail, life moved on, and without noticing anything was happening our group were learning things, through questions and the "old monkey see monkey do," or, in other words, "Bloody well do as you are told." Or "How many times do you need to be shown?" I found that the people I respected, and indeed learned more from, were not the loud "do as you are told" brigade, but the men that took the time to show us how it was done by example. However, there wasn't too many of this ilk as most had been brought up the old, hard way, and thought this was the way to show these young buggers. Even later as I became a fireman, the old hard men would drive the engines as hard as they could, just so you were kept in line and knew your place.

Often, when I should have been cleaning an engine or brushing a floor, I would sneak quietly into one or other of the old bothies (these were small concrete buildings where the engine drivers and their mates would wait for the engines to return from wherever, to be re-coaled and their fires cleaned.) On the roster this was called engine disposal. I would listen to the older generation, some of them were really enlightening with their tales, no doubt added to each time of telling. Tales of their trains running late and what daring-do they undertook to get back on time, of weather conditions similar to the Arctic. Was this déjà-vu? I could have been sitting in the corner of Tom Fishers barbers shop in Water St. as a young boy listening to the tales of the well-informed clients that seemed to dwell there, and Tom master of ceremonies keeping everyone right.

CHAPTER 18

Winter turned to spring and early summer. An abiding memory was the Caledonian Express, it was the latest venture of the West Coast battle with the East Coast to have the best, the fastest, the most up to date express on British Rail. The Caledonian was to cover the four hundred miles from Glasgow to London in four hundred minutes. The inaugural run was something to be seen, this magnificent one hundred ton, sparkling engine pulling equally sparkling carriages, roared past Kingmoor to a rapturous applause from a great gathering of workers from the shed. The engine crew must have been told of, or were expecting, the reception because as it passed the cheering crowd, the driver hung onto the whistle until the train was almost out of sight. The expression on the fireman's face said it all – "look at me, am I not the cat's whiskers?" The steam, the smoke and the sound of the speeding train is something I can still remember with great pride and affection. It was also the only time I can recall the shed master not asking everyone "do you lot have nothing to do, because I can soon find you something."

The first six months of my working life had passed so quickly it was like a blur, I had cycled the twelve miles or so to work on a lot of occasions. More than a few times I'd had to get a lift when the bike needed a new tyre, lacked brakes or something else. I now knew how to hold a shovel and which end of a brush to hold, but I was still not an engine driver. The audacity of youth had still not learned to accept a little thing called patience.

I had a uniform befitting a member of the footplate staff, but was only allowed on the footplate at the invitation of (for want of a better word) the grownups. If I had occasion to get a lift on the massive engine that trundled back and forth to the station, I always felt the glow, the excitement of what I thought was being grown up. And the opportunity of leaning over the side of a live engine as it progressed through the station, where it was obvious that the passengers on the platform realised that I was part of this great unit, hissing steam and smoke, smelling of hot ash and hot oil. They must have been in awe of this young man on the footplate.

Summer was something else, beside the heat from the engines, the ash and the smoke, the sun seemed to shine all the time and there was no escape. Inside the shed it was constantly twilight, the sweat ran, found its way into every crease in my skin and along with the sweat, of course, went the coal dust, the only clean part of me and my work mates was our lips. As we dehydrated, our tongues would run around our lips and thereby keep them clean. It was a constant back and forward to the wash room for water. The condition of the sinks and the taps left a lot to be desired, how anyone never caught any disease I will never know. There was someone supposed to keep the place in some sort of order, but he had health problems and used these as a constant excuse for not being able to keep the place, at least, tidy. Scrupulous was out of the question and was a word which I am sure he couldn't spell, let alone carry out. The odd thing about the toilets was, that not one of the doors had locks on, and any sort of privacy could only be attained by wedging folded newspaper or cotton waste between door and jamb. Most of the older men would simply sit with the door open and their newspaper on their knee, reading whilst everyone else went about their own business. With no one taking a blind bit of notice, other than when a particular colleague passed by it would be " Hi Bill, how's it going." Or "Are you going to sit there all day." The obvious retort being "Bugger off."

The last time I could remember being as hot and dusty was a good few years previously. When me and my trusty companion, Dai, found we had nothing to do or lacked funds for the pictures, we could be found in Water St. Along the road from Tom Fishers was a row of old back to back cottages.

Doorless, windowless and not much in the way of floors, (these had probably been rescued as fire wood in years past). It was not beyond the whit of young lads to find a way into the attic space.

On one particular day, the two of us had managed to get to the far end of this almost derelict building and were on our way back to where we had climbed inside. One, or both, of us must have stood on a rotten beam and with a crack it gave way, spilling us into a black void. "Hell what happened?" my accomplice gasped. "How the hell do I know!" "Where are we?" It was impossible to see your hand in front of your face it was so dark.

The only light came from the hole we had just made in the ceiling. The question came just as another shaft of light appeared below us and in the light, we could make out a shadow, at that same moment as seeing the shadow, a not too happy voice made a funny request. "What the bloody hell is going on." The disembodied voice I recognised, but could make nothing of the shadow now enveloped in a cascade of dust. The voice belonged to Willie Baba, at least that is what his nickname was. Most, if not all, of the male population in the town had a nickname and it was difficult to recollect any of their given names. Of course, there wasn't the politically correct group about in those far off days, which was just as well, because the whole lot of them would have had apoplexy.

Our scrabbling about and the sound must have alerted Willie that all was not well, and he had opened the door to what turned out to be a narrow staircase, my pal and I were perched on the landing half way up. Now I have never been a one to hang about to find out what was going to happen next and grabbing my pals arm I simply said, "Come on quick." We were down the few steps and into his living room. The front door was open and was the source of the light on the staircase as the sun shone through the opening. As we exited the building most of the dust we had caused followed in our wake. Willie had obviously not yet grasped what had happened and watched as we left like two mini whirlwinds. I can't print any of the language that followed our flight down the street, but it was colourful to say the least. I can say that some of the words were "I know who you are and I know your fathers, just you wait till I get my hands on you, you little varmints. Unfortunately, Willie must have had polio or some accident in his past and finished up with a permanently bent leg. To compensate for this disability someone had made him what I can only describe as a large u shaped piece of steel which was fitted to his boot. The only adjustment to this appendage was a piece of wood that formed a rough sole and needed to be changed from time to time to compensate for any wear. Neither of us thought to stop until we reached the end of the street. Once there, feeling a little safer, I ventured a look back, the dust was still billowing out of the house and had, by now, attracted a crowd all eager to find out what had happened. From where I was, it looked like the whole of the inside of the building had collapsed. Home is the place to be right now I remember thinking, setting off at a brisk pace toward a place of safety.

Every time we were in bother, we waited in dread for the next few weeks but nothing happened, however it was some time before either of us ventured into the confines of Water St.

The whole group of us new boys were made aware that we would not be officially allowed on the footplate until we were sixteen plus. Why? Well this was British Rail and it was in the rule book, and every person on the footplate staff had to abide by this Bible of the railway. Time was approaching when us juniors would have to sit an exam of sorts; not an exam in the true meaning of the word, mostly this involved sitting in a dingy room being fed information and then answering questions. This was to see if we were to become firemen or, to be more precise, passed cleaners of the future.

As we approached late autumn some of us were required to attend classes. As each of us booked on one Monday morning, Joe Strong, the time keeper, informed each of us that our presence would be required in what could be described as the classroom, up the stairs above the Shed master's office. Each of us had different ideas of what was instore for us, because at the mention of exams it was a shock, like being back at school and we all knew what exams at school were like. I do remember one lad saying, "Bloody hell I'll never pass; I can hardly write my own name." It wasn't going to be at all like any of us thought! We were actually treated as grownups.

At the given time, we assembled outside the office under the large clock, and for the first time we met our instructor, Joe Armstrong. He was to be our mentor and would decide if any of us would make the grade to Passed Cleaner. It turned out that Joe had been on the footplate but for some reason he had been elevated to an inspector.

My God what a step up to be a Passed Cleaner and we would get a pay rise as well! Always providing we made the grade. Not until a later date did any of us find out that whether we'd failed or not. After an allotted time the exam could be taken again. So it was only a matter of time before everyone got through.

'Classroom' was a misnomer if ever there was one, it was a dingy room with a few tables and chairs, and the lighting was supplied by two, one candle power, light bulbs - both could have made a difference if the soot and grime had been washed off them. Everything matched, it was all colour coordinated with a nice covering of soot, and an undertone of nicotine, even the cobwebs were the same colour and were obviously installed at the same time as the building was put up. Some bright spark had written in the grime on the window the old war time saying. "Wot, no Bananas?" With the bald-headed, large nosed man peering over the top of a wall. No one had made any attempt to remove the graffiti as this was the railway and the railway had rules and the railway had unions and this was always someone else's job, so there it stayed.

We were obviously grown-up as there was no attempt, by any of us, to ask if it was alright to smoke. Those who were lucky enough to have fags were immediately preyed up on by those who didn't. There was a lot of scrabbling of chairs being pushed and pulled around until everyone got settled. "Come on we haven't got all day." It was Joe (our mentor for the following few weeks) who managed to bring a little quiet to the gathering. (For anyone reading this I should like to point out that many swear words and expletives were part of daily language on BR but I have left them out of the narrative and left it up to each reader to decide what they would be.) This first day turned out to be not too bad at all. It was the first time in ages that each of us wasn't covered in oil and although we still had a certain amount of dirt and dust on our persons, it was nothing compared to what would normally be covering overalls and skin alike. At bait time, as it was known, we all trooped out for a break. there was much banter and leg pulling, mostly I think, to ease the tension, and as youngster's no-one would admit to being one bit bothered - I think it is called "bravado."

Some that were lucky enough to have money or a slate in the canteen. (Only the lads that had been at the shed for some- time and were able to prove they would pay up on pay day.) Headed off at high speed to get to the front of the queue for a tuppenny Woodbine and a cuppa. The women that ran the canteen were mostly good natured and could be relied on to supply fags. (Cigarettes.) on tick until the weekend. Not much of a range of food only the proper railway sandwiches ham or cheese with the turned- up edges and the extra crusty crusts. Occasionally when they remembered or could be bothered there would be boiled eggs and other staple BR commodities. Bottles of tomato and brown sauce lids held in place with the requisite amount of gunge always had centre stage on each table. Salt and pepper only when the thief that waylaid the pots returned them empty hoping for a refill before taking them home again. Nothing was ever really clean, even after being washed down the tables were still sticky and streaky.

This was all new and some of it unbelievable. The rest of us would make do with the cabin and our day to day rations. I counted myself lucky with what I had in my bait, some of the lads for whatever reason didn't have anything in the way of food, various reasons were offered some would say they had forgotten their bait, or were not hungry, however the same lads would be happy to help out with anyone else's sandwiches. I sometimes felt sorry for one or two of the lads as it was obvious they didn't have much and maybe nothing at home either the way they looked coming to work almost as if they hadn't bothered to wash since last time they were on duty. Their overalls not washed from one week to the next and sitting next to one of them there would be the stale smell of sweat and soot. But it was never wise to mention this. I was always happy to share what I had and became quite popular at bait time. There was however a couple of lads that would take advantage and were almost into my bait as quickly as I was, and it was the same pair that never had cigarettes. Eventually everyone became sick of what was really scrounging as they never reciprocated and after a few weeks they were quietly put in their place after trying to bully one of the lads into giving them his last ciggy.

There was a long-standing induction for new starters which involved the new starter being debagged, and his private parts liberally coated in engine oil and smokebox ash ground well in. These two were the first in our batch. All of us enjoyed the spectacle little knowing that in a short time we would follow suit. It was impossible to avoid this inauguration and much better to get it over with as soon as possible the alternative was having to go through with it a second time. Believe me the whole process was at least embarrassing as I can vouch. The trip home on the train was at best uncomfortable if not embarrassing as the train was full and I found it difficult to scratch the itches without anyone noticing. My mother thought this was barbaric and should be stopped my dad thought it funny and was about to relate what had happened to him when he went into the army, but a quick glower from mam changed his mind and he just kept on smiling. Good old dad.

My Mother was ahead of her times in a lot of ways, as was my father for that matter. Throughout the war mother repaired mosquito airplanes for the RAF at the local airfield and had all her own opinions, which she was never afraid to air. My dad came back from the war and mended his own clothes, polished everyone's boots and could be counted upon to put a hot home cooked casserole on the table for the whole family. His cooking was even better than mams! No such thing as women's work, there was only work, if it needed doing then it didn't matter who did it, as long as it was done. Just as it should be. However, there was that one time when my mother almost caused a murder...

My Mother was good friends with Annie (I won't use her real name). Annie occasionally visited our house, as people seemed to do in those days, almost always with the same greeting "Are you in? It's only me." On a few occasions their exchange of gossip would take place in the living room, and little boys were usually dispatched to do nothing in particular, they were just told to go out and play. As it turned out, Annie's husband, after he had had a few drinks could be violent with her and would leave her with bruises for all to see. Annie would invariably end up in our living room, bruised and shaking for my mother to comfort. Annie would sit, drinking her tea, obviously devastated. Being only a boy I couldn't understand what all the commotion was for.

After a couple of visits mam couldn't help herself but say, "Annie, you are daft for putting up with it, if it was me I would wait until the great fat b***d is asleep, pull the blankets over his head and batter him with whatever is to hand". To be perfectly honest, she would be just the woman to do that too, domestic violence had no place in her world and it pained her greatly to see it in others.

All this had been a week or two previous and now Annie was sitting shaking once again in our living room. "Mamie!" (The name all the neighbours called my mam.) "I think I've killed him, I did as you said and after he had gone to bed I pulled the blanket over his head and hit him, I couldn't stop."

"Bloody hell, lass, what did you hit him with?"

"The frying pan, maybe I shouldn't have, because I can't waken him."

I am not exactly too sure about what happened next, but the crack was all around Wigton, her husband couldn't get up for days, and it was getting on for weeks before he could go out. Annie had given him such a beating. Never again did he lay a finger on his tiny wife and could be seen regularly carrying her groceries home for her.

CHAPTER 19

Over the years I was privy to visit many different engine sheds up and down the country, one thing stuck in my mind – the tea urns were all the same grotty colour, a colourist would call it deep chestnut or dark oak. However, there was no getting away from it, they were all hacky, but if they had been cleaned would the tea still taste the same? Most of the cups and mugs were of the same colour, some were maybe a little different in that they had cracks you could almost see through, maybe the owner had been in one of the sand boxes, and by giving it a good scrub with sand and water given it a new lease of life.

The training side was boring stuck inside the grotty office, but we wouldn't make the grade as Passed Cleaners unless we attended. We had to learn the rules set out in the black covered rule book, everyone had to have one. Strange, but the only one I can remember was rule 55 – When in fog and falling snow to the signal box you must go – this was the fireman's (or in our case, possibly a past cleaner.) This was to remind the signalman of where the train was standing at a particular signal, and so avoid any collisions.

Anyway the weeks passed, and at the end of the training we were presented to the shed master for questions. I must admit, (but never to the other lads, after all I needed to maintain a little kudos) it was more than a bit daunting standing in front of Mr Darcy. (I was always of the opinion that he would have made a better undertaker than a shed master.) I was convinced that our leader, the shed master, didn't really want to be involved with us, let's face it a bunch of scruffy Herbert's. He would ask a question and then he seemed to drift off, I am not entirely sure if he ever heard the answer, but in my case, it didn't matter for as soon as he could, I was passed and dismissed. Maybe it was lunchtime for him. Most of the motley crew passed ok, but one or two were required to go through the whole scenario again. For us lucky ones there was, of course, much praising of one another and comments of "easy really!" Don't forget this was British rail and you should put your own interpretation and include a few! No not a few, a lot, of swear words in here.

The world was our oyster, now we would visit exotic places such as Glasgow, Leeds, Hellifield and wondrous other destinations and without any cost! The best thing was we all got a raise from forty-two shillings and six pence to a staggering one hundred and twelve shillings a week, a king's ransom! Mam of course got half, but the rest was my own to spend as I wished, and for a penniless boy it was indeed a fortune.

Now for the next big step. Although we could be acting firemen as required, we weren't allowed on the main line or passenger trains until we had gained a certain amount of experience and had to acquire a number of turns a they were called. Days on local work such as shunting and hauling goods trains from one yard to another. Again, enthusiasm didn't count and as a young man, lacking patience, it took forever to gather the necessary turns required before moving on to greater things

We were now allowed to work night shift as well as working daytime. This meant we were obliged to meet up somewhere before the shift and the simplest place was the Redfern, a real railway pub. Being sixteen was not a deterrent, the uniform gave each one of us the right to a pint same as all the other footplate men. I can't remember a time when I was ever challenged about my age, but it was obvious to everyone we were all new to the inside of a public house. But true to form we all tried to look as if we belonged there.

A pint of mild was eleven pence, a pint of mixed a shilling and a pint of bitter one shilling and a penny. Not to look such a novice to the group standing at the bar, I had decided that I would ask for whatever the fireman in front of me asked for. The barman smiled when he asked what I wanted, "A pint of bitter", and was still smiling as he pulled my first ever pint of bitter. (I have to admit I still like a pint of bitter.) Being a Passed Cleaner brought with it the need to adopt a different attitude in appearance, there were no written rules it was just expected, polished boots, clean overalls and of course polished cap, most of us did it.

Whenever we had to relieve another crew we would almost always be given directions, via one pub or another. I still do the same to this day, although it's getting more difficult with the number of pubs now closed. It soon became a pre-requisite to have a pint before shift, it was to replace all the sweat we would lose on the footplate. Everyone I knew gave that as a valid reason, with one exception, and that was after shift, now the pint or so was to replace the sweat we had lost during the shift. Ah, the good old days! This was a new era, instead of being a scruffy head to toe cleaner, smelling of paraffin and soot, it was now expected to turn up for work in at least a presentable fashion. The older generation of drivers didn't hold back when telling you how "it might be better for all if YOU MADE A BLOODY EFFORT". After all soap and water was cheap. Most lads did without being told but a few, even years after, would look the same coming on shift as they had looked going home after shift. One in particular spent all his hard-earned pay packet on the horses. He never seemed to care how he looked, he was one of the lads that never had any bait and would happily pick up whatever anyone left. It was sad because he was very bright and knew far more than the rest of us put together. I understood that he had a very good education and came from, what you would call, a very good family, there was a rumour he could have gone to Oxford. A few months after becoming a passed cleaner, I was sent on my bike to tell this lad he would be needed for an early morning job. I eventually found the address, it turned out to be a cellar. After a minute or two banging on the door, it swung open and the lad in question stood there in his entire work garb except his cap, he even had his boots on. I informed him about the job, he simply nodded and closed the door. I climbed the cellar steps quite shaken. I couldn't believe my eyes, got back on my bike and made my way back to the shed. The foreman looked as I came through the office door. "Well? is he coming in or not?" Not knowing what to say, I simply replied." All he said was yes and closed the door." I didn't feel as if I was telling lies really, as he did nod in reply.

After the first year overalls became pale blue with constant washing, instead of the navy blue when they were issued and a lot of firemen took great pride in how they turned out for work, while others, well - I reserve judgment.

My first main line trip was totally unexpected, a fireman had failed to book on and next in line was me. For the driver, it was an everyday thing, but for me it was special. When I told him it was my first main line job, he laughed, and told me not to worry. In an effort to make an impression, I simply replied I wasn't worried. He laughed some more. "I'm sure we'll manage" he smiled and went about preparing the engine for this, (to me) a very special day. Whatever I do, whatever I say, this day will be with me for the rest of my life. The excitement the nerves, the exhilaration, the apprehension, was something else and try as I might I couldn't get rid of the smile that kept coming over my face. I checked the tool bucket, shovel, etc.etc. from the stores, having had to first give the engine number and the job number to the little storeman with the big ego. I built the fire just as I had been shown over the past few weeks and months. Checked the injectors were both working again, as I had also been shown. Made sure all the fire irons were in place. Hell! Never mind the last few weeks and months, this was the real thing, this was my first trip on the main line. It may have been on just a goods train but that didn't matter. I felt as if I should shout out of the cab window, but I was a grown up now maybe that wouldn't be the thing to do. So I just kept on smiling and preparing this almost living thing for the job of work expected of it.

I may have mentioned it before and no doubt will again as my story unravels. The smell of the hot oil, the fumes from the firebox, the steam finding its way through any gap it could just to prove it was alive. It didn't have to prove any such thing to this lad, I knew it was alive, I could feel it. "Take it down to the water tower". My driver said as he collected his billy can. "I'll go and fill this, then when you have the tank full you can get yours done". Without a moment's hesitation, he clambered down the steps and off into the bothy.

I can't say this was the first time I had driven a hundred odd ton locomotive, but this was the first time that it was to be legitimate, (well partly legitimate). That is how it happened in those far off days. Health and safety was a far off something in the mists of time. If it had existed then, the world would have come to a stop. I am in no way burying my head in the sand, but I do believe the people who impose these rules and regulations have never had a real job, maybe that is part of their problem. But I digress, this very large piece of brilliant mechanical engineering needed a drink and that was my job at that moment.

The feeling took me back to the day I first learned how to ride a bike. There were hardly any kids' bikes in those far-off days, only the occasional three wheelers and, given the opportunity, most of the kids I was growing up with would take turns to have a ride. That is, until the parent of the young owner of the bike appeared on the scene and scattered us to our various abodes. The day arrived when my dad was out and, would you believe it, his bike was left at the back door. As one or two of my playmates were about it wasn't long until it was decided that it would be a good idea to take it for a spin, even though none of us could ride. As it was my dad's bike I would try first and with someone holding the seat and someone else holding me we gave it a try on the back-cinder path. Not a good idea as cinders really dig into your skin especially your knees, elbows were no better, and black ash combined with blood do not look good nor does it feel good either. We had only been out for a few minutes when my dad's voice interrupted the game. My pals were not really my pals, as I turned to where they had been standing just seconds earlier looking for their support, there was no one there! They were already rounding the corner at the end of the block, not even a backward glance to see how I fared. Caught in the act, it wasn't worth saying anything in mitigation as the blood and the cinders were a dead giveaway, as were the now twisted handlebars. Not a great deal of damage was caused, but to me it was like the start of a world war and only the blood and cinders saved me from certain death. As the bike was rescued and the handlebars were straightened, it came to me that maybe a few tears might help the situation, a mistake! "You can cry lad but wait till you get in the house. How do you think I am going to get into work eh?" Good old mam saved the waif "Tom, the bike will mend, fetch that boy in till we can see what he has managed to do to himself this time." I wasn't really hurt and I am sure the tears helped. After the cinders were washed off there were only a few scrapes and a couple of bruises. But the bike remained a no-go area for now.

A few days later my dad must have had a rethink or maybe mam had said something to stir him into teaching me to ride. Please remember, in those far off days, there was no such thing as stabilisers for bicycles! A second consideration was the size of the bike. It was a full-sized man's bike and a youngster of my stature could make no attempt at getting my leg over the cross bar and that was not the only complication. To ride this steed, I needed both hands on the handlebars and at the same time be able to use the brakes, such as they were. Added to the mix I needed to be able to steer the damned thing without my feet slipping from the pedals. This position for a grown up would have been difficult but almost impossible for me, almost! It seemed to take forever but maybe it was only a couple of days before my dad finally let go of the seat and shouted "you're on your own now."

Elation, terror, awesome, a freedom never to be forgotten. So this is how my long affair with what at the time was a freedom unparalleled and got me into no end of trouble because, as soon as my dad's bike was left unattended it would disappear. There was no use ever trying to lie my way out of taking it, as my right leg and sock were forever covered in black oil from the chain. That bike and me were hardly apart, except when I allowed my dad to use it to go to work on! I really needed a bike of my own – however that was a long way in the future.

Bicycles were a major form of transport for anyone lucky enough to have one. And it was not unusual to see as many as thirty or forty piled on top of each other in Stampers garage. These pedal powered means of transport would be left by the women who worked at Redmayne's tailors, how they managed to get the right bike after work I often wondered! I am not sure if the owners of the bicycles paid Mr. Stamper anything for the space to leave them while they were at work. But I am sure that he would have been on the right side, as all the girls would bring in the accumulators – an early form of battery – out of the wireless at home to be recharged. There was a large red machine with dials and pointers on the front, in the corner of the garage, to which each accumulator would be attached with wires. It stood there looking as if it wasn't doing anything really, it only hummed like a huge swarm of bees so it must have been doing something as the large square glass jars, filled with some kind of liquid, were changed quite often before being collected by the owners.

Electric drills were as rare as hens back teeth but there was a solution to most things. My dad was quite practical in some ways, and if he needed a hole in a piece of wood, he would simply put the poker in the fire until it was red hot and use it to burn a hole. It was good to watch as the poker was twisted this way and that until eventually there was the hole, flames and all. Although it quite often needed the poker to be returned to the fire to reheat more than once. Using this solution to hole drilling it was possible to help with the manufacture of a trolley, or soap box as it was known in posh circles. The wheels and axles would come from the local tip and the wood would be scrounged from the fruit shop or the Co-op. Odd times it would be possible to acquire a Co-op delivery box, but that could cause a world war if caught, and no mitigating circumstances would appease the co-op manager! The hole drilling was needed for the front axle, a hole in the main frame and a hole to match in the cross bar. A rusty old bolt and nut to join the two pieces and it was possible to steer the thing, in a lot of cases not very accurately but good enough to avoid most collisions.

I have personally suffered quite a bit of, what was commonly known as, gravel rash from parting company with a trolley, on a downhill descent. A wheel that had previously been attached to the axle by means of a bent nail, or a piece of twisted wire, may just have chosen to leave the vehicle without warning. Possibly the rusty nut and bolt would part company with one another, thereby leaving no alternative but to come to a grinding halt at best, at worst pieces of skin would be left on the gravel and pieces of gravel left in their place. A totally unacceptable situation for the driver, but it was a frequent occurrence and usually required the vehicle to be dragged home for running repairs.

Saturday morning and it fell to me to go to the Co-op for some shopping and having just built a "new" trolley it had to go with me. Not much in the way of hills to descend on the way into town. I had a plan. After collecting the provisions and stowed them on board, going straight home was never a part of my plan. I would take the long way home and that would allow me to test the speed of the trolley down baths hill. First, I had to pull the thing up one side before the test run down the other side.

Everything was well on the uphill part, now I could climb on board and let it go.

The first part of the downhill was going great, the shopping jogging about behind me, the wheels doing the hokey-cokey wobbling from side to side, my hair blowing in the slipstream. The cord attached to the front axle was held in place with a couple of wire staples. At this point I should tell anyone making a trolley, don't use staples to fix the steering – it is not always successful.

I couldn't believe it, I had the cord in my hand but the end that should have been attached to the steering wasn't where it should be. It was dragging underneath. No steering, no brakes and before I could think, the trolley made up its own mind and headed for the wall. Cartwheels are good on a cart, but no good at all sitting on a trolley doing its own thing. Groceries that should have been safely in the back, were now in a contest with me on who could do the most cartwheels. Butter and sugar destined for the family table would now not make it.

Eventually coming to a halt, the trolley was now in the various parts that I had started with, only now they were strewn, along with the groceries and a fair amount of my skin, on the grass verge. Elbows, knuckles, chin and knees, all vying for attention, which to rub first, which not to rub at all. Rubbing damaged parts of my anatomy while trying to pick up flattened bits of butter that were now part of the road, bread in a totally different guise to what it was meant to be. Parts of my trolley scattered with everything else. In my heart I knew it was going to be the groceries that would give me most grief. It was going to be a day when I would need to lean on my obvious injuries, maybe even making out just how life threatening they were.

This was not one of my better days, in fact at that moment it was my worst day ever. And I had not yet thought about the problems I would have when I got home.

On a warm day bacon and butter don't really mix very well and maybe I should have given more thought before piling everything in a heap, in the remnants of my trolley. The idea was to drag the whole heap home where, with a little bit of repair, it might resemble what had started out as a trolley full of shopping. It was never going to happen.

As I set off dragging the ex-trolley homeward, little bits of the shopping began to slide off with the vibration. Every few yards I had to stop and retrieve whatever. This was not going to work, and I needed to appease my mam with a good excuse as to why the shopping was in such a state. Most of it fitted into a large brown paper bag, maybe that was a bad idea? What didn't fit in the bag could be tucked into my jumper if I pushed the bottom of it in my trouser belt. Sensible? Or was it? I would hurry home with the groceries and come back for my trolley.

Baths hill was not a busy place, so no one would nick it if I hurried. I had not considered the long-term effect it was to have on all sorts of things. Pictures - they were out for a start. No pocket money - but that was a non-starter because I never got any. No dinner - well I wasn't home ever on time to get any, unless it was in the oven after which I needed a hammer and chisel to pry it from the plate. I was just trying to make myself feel better but without any success. Things just got worse as I got nearer to home.

Maybe I shouldn't go directly home, maybe I should stay out until tea time. Out of the question, the family would be waiting for the, now butter soaked, bacon for dinner. Nothing for it, get home and hope my injuries outweighed the damage to the shopping!

For a few moments after going into the kitchen through the back door I was in luck, mam went into a flap when she saw the wounds I had managed to inflict on my flight with my trolley. That was to change as she washed the grit from my knees to see how bad the damage was. "Where's the shopping." She asked as an aside to my trolley. "Outside." I tried to be a little casual. That was not working as my mam looked up from the sink, which was now taking on a pinkish colour as a mixture of blood and grit was removed from my skin. I was right about some things - no pictures, no pocket money, but that was as usual. What I couldn't grasp, was how calm my mother seemed at the time.

Cuts and bruises clean of gravel, face washed, but trying to limp on both legs at the same time did not work. "Right get back to the shop and get everything you have managed to destroy, and you'd better hurry, your dad will finish work at two, I don't know what he will say about this."

"But mam I can hardly walk. Can't somebody else go."

"I don't care if you have to crawl, you had better be back before your dad gets in."

Dad asked all sorts of difficult questions that afternoon but funnily, he never mentioned groceries. For the next few days I worried about just when he would raise the subject. He was concerned enough about my injuries because he said on more than one occasion, words to the effect that maybe it would teach me a lesson and I would make sure things were fixed properly before venturing out on to the road.

I still wasn't sure about the groceries and it had almost been pushed from my mind, when my mam asked me to go up street for something. Before I could winge and look for an excuse, she quietly reminded me that I owed her a favour as she hadn't said a word about the fiasco with the trolley and the shopping.

It was then that I knew that this was going to be a long drawn out favour, but there was very little I could do until my mam thought the favour was paid in full.

CHAPTER 20

The hand brake was on the tender and with a little effort I turned the wheel that operated it, crossed to the controls on the other side of the cab, the forward and reverse control turned easily, like the well-oiled piece of machinery it was, my hand on the regulator this was it! A gentle pull was all that was needed before the giant breathed steam from the open cylinders. As an after-thought I took the liberty of blowing the whistle. (I should have done that first but everyone needs to learn.) Very easily the engine slipped quietly forward, steam alternating first from one cylinder then the other. Moving almost imperceptibly, I could feel the raw power, exhilarating, exciting, what else? Well everything else that's what, this was amazing, the water tower slid past and I closed the regulator and brought the beast to a halt. Thankfully my first outing with the engine went a little bit more smoothly than my earlier experiments with makeshift vehicles.

Becoming a Passed Cleaner brought with it a whole new set of responsibilities. As young irresponsible people, we felt that we did have a certain responsibility - to make sure that each individual pub would benefit from our regular patronage, this was to prove, in most part, a smashing part of my life. At sixteen and while wearing the BR uniform it proved to be a simple task, as the uniform or rather the overalls, of a footplate man would open doors and answer questions almost before they were asked. I honestly cannot remember being asked my age by mine host of any licenced premises. A quizzical look from time to time but never outright "are you eighteen?" This part of my life I remember with happy thoughts, and with the odd laugh at friends older than me being asked to prove their age. As a matter of fact, one of our group always carried his birth certificate, a wrong move in many cases, as the landlord would think this is a smart arse and just for the hell of it, he would be evicted without a pint. Albeit with a lot of fuss, and a lot of "This isn't fair. I am older than any of these guys," at which point we would all be ejected post haste.

Under circumstances like this we always had a friend who, although he would deny it if asked, could not hold his drink, and was from time to time a source of great amusement to us young dare anything teenagers. A particular night being in a pub called the Sun. Everything was good until Loggie had to go to the toilet, he was gone for ages and we decided we should go and find him. He was where he had set off to go only he was on his knees talking to the toilet bowl. Although I don't remember the conversation, it seemed Loggie meant every word, because when we tried to extricate him from that position (wrapped around the bowl), he was having none of it until he had finished his conversation, and as he was a big strong lad it took time. We did eventually manage it, just before the land lord appeared and so avoided all and sundry being given a lifetime ban.

Loggie was a big lad and, as we had all been promised to have seats kept for us in the local cinema (obviously by young attractive girls), there was no way we would get past the usher with him in this state and a solution was called for and quickly. Across the road from the Sun was the auction and a quick scout around the yard unveiled a roofing ladder propped against the wall. What a find! It was decided that if we could put one arm in part of the ladder and the other arm in the opposite rung he would be suspended in a more or less upright stance, and we could all slope of to the pictures and pick him up later. Good idea (for us) maybe not so good for Loggie.

Just before the last bus arrived it was brought to everyone's notice we had not retrieved the poor lad. "All together lads, lift," was the command. We all strained to remove the captive from the rungs, it was not as easy as we thought. He had been held in that position for far too long and when we did finally retrieve him, he could hardly stand and needed to shuffle along with more than two of us helping, and he still resembled the hunch back of Notre Dame. This had been the easy bit, getting the conductor of the bus to let him on was a lesson in diplomacy, and only then because the conductor happened to know "Tom Scott's boy", were any of us allowed to get on before the vehicle departed, after all they did have a time table to run too.

Poor Loggie's hunch back lasted for ages and maybe it wasn't quite pc, but we did take a rise out of the lad whenever we met up. It's a good job he had a good sense of humour and he wore the jibes with his great smile.

It was to be my eldest brother's wedding and my pal, Dai, and myself were asked to be ushers, whatever that meant but by all accounts it was an honour. It also meant I had to have a suit for the occasion and not one "off the peg". My aunt Ginny worked at Redmayne's tailors who were always supposed to be one of the best in the land. They made suits for the landed gentry and for the Royal family, for which they were awarded The Royal Warrant. Although now just a shadow of its past history, I think they still maintain this award. An appointment was made to be measured, although everyone knew the family connection it wasn't needed. Mr Carrick, a proper gent, would do the measuring. He measured this way and that, then I was asked to stand up straight with my legs slightly apart. All well and good, then after measuring my inside leg I was asked the question. "Which side does sir dress on." Being from a simple country background I had to think carefully, then it dawned on me I got out of bed on the right side, so this must be what Mr. Carrick was eluding to. "Right side Mr. Carrick". I replied. "Good, good", was all he said. It was years later, when on a similar venture in Luper's of Camden, (they were the tailors the tv stars supported, it was just up the road from the ITV studio's), it actually struck me what good old Mr. Carrick had meant! I wonder if he realised then, what I had just realised? My new suit fitted like a glove, pale grey with a raindrop effect. I hadn't wanted turn-ups on the trousers, however my aunt had been informed that "Your nephews suit is on the cutting table", and as everyone in the town knew everyone, I am surprised it did not appear in the local press. My suit arrived for a fitting and guess what! The suit had turn ups and it was wanted in the next week, so I had turn ups didn't I?

My aunt was devious and as far as I can remember she would find a way to get her own way. When I was about to go to secondary modern school every boy of my age got to wear long trousers. My mam had bought me a pair of long grey flannels for my new venture and I was chuffed. Not my aunt – for almost two days she visited our house and went on and on until my mam gave in and returned the trousers and replaced them with short ones. I was in tears, what would the rest of my school pals say, they would have at least a long laugh about them. I did everything an eleven year old could do, threatened never to go to school, run away where they would never find me, never ever do any shopping no sticks, nothing. It didn't work though, my aunt had her way and on my first school day at the secondary modern I, with two other pupils, wore short trousers. I don't think I ever forgave her for that. Well, maybe the odd time when I was desperately in need of money for the pictures.

A useful coincidence in my youth was, that the only windows in the home of my Grandmother McPherson overlooked a cobbled yard. The other side of the yard was the rear of the Palace cinema where the people who worked there could gain access, through a doorway onto Meetinghouse Lane. There were a few steps up to the projection room and a doorway that lead into the cinema under a staircase.

On days when there was no money to be had to gain entry, I had a little ploy. The window in the living room was level with the surface of the yard and by sliding the sash window up it was an easy matter to slip into the yard on the pretence of helping my big brother Norman to rewind the used film onto another spool ready for further use. He happened to be one of the projectionists at that time, along with Frank Ingledow and Jimmy Bulman. Jimmy was a good guy and played along with the freebee entry after I had wound a few spools. Frank was a different kettle of fish and did nothing to help my free entry. I think his officious nature may have had something to do with being an Air Raid Warden during the war. He was unfortunate enough to be hung on a lamp post by his braces for being so officious on one occasion, or so I believe!

Another part of the coincidence was that my sister Mary got a job at the Palace and took the tickets. She was also responsible for the sale of ice cream during the interval. Need I say more? The only way it could have been better in those few years was if the family had owned the cinema.

Life was never humdrum, it was never the same two days in a row, always something going on, book on at the station or maybe a job at Durranhill for a goods train to Settle. To some people this was a pain in the neck, but to me it was just what I needed, never the same thing. One particular day, I had to be at Kingmoor as fireman on a dead engine. (I know you might ask "Why a fireman on an engine with no fire?" I am not entirely sure myself but I suspect it was in case the hand brake had to be applied or something.) The engine had to be dragged to St Rollox in Glasgow for major repairs as it had been involved in an accident and the repairs were too big to be done at Carlisle. It happened that a good friend of mine was on the towing engine and as we were unable to travel at any speed we would be put into a suitable siding to allow express passenger trains, or fully fitted goods past, and it took absolute ages to travel a few miles without having to stop. It was at one of these stops that I realised I had left my bait at the shed when I booked on. I wasn't hungry until then and the more I thought about it the hungrier I became. We were put inside at a place called Carstairs to allow the evening passenger trains to pass. I climbed down and made it to the front engine just as the crew were having their sandwiches.

The two men looked at me I think they knew what my problem was but neither of them spoke. I had to ask didn't I "Any spare?" It had to be asked, I was starving. "I have left my bloody bait at the shed." My old pal smiled "No, I haven't." His driver looked over at me, "Nope not a thing." "Bloody hell I'll never make it to Glasgow." I said. "Ian my old pal, have you nothing left at all?" He pulled his sandwich box from his haversack as if to show me it was empty. Inside nestled a great big tea cake. "Will that be any good?" He asked. "Bloody hell will it be any good," was my reply!

No by your leave, nor please or thank you, I reached into his box and extricated the thing of beauty and, in the same movement, pushed a huge part of it in my watering mouth. "Never tasted anything like it." I said as the last morsel disappeared. Smiles all round. "Best teacake I've ever had! What was in it?" I put the question to my pal. "Sandwich spread," he informed me "I'm glad you liked it, I'm a bit sick of it myself." A quick mouthful of the treacle like tea from the hot plate over the firebox and it was back to my post. One thing from that trip haunted me for weeks to come. I made the mistake of telling my mother about this feast, guess what I got in my bait for the next few months?

"Hey Scotty, know how to use a phone?" I immediately thought this was a trap and responded, "Nah, only phone I know is at the top of our road." The question was asked by my foreman Ernie Heron. "Good, now is the time for you to learn. They want someone in the office to man the phones, you'll do." No use trying to argue with him, I did manage to splutter a few expletive's, along with not being able to work inside or I wasn't cut out to be an office boy. Ernie had already disappeared back through the office door and I was expected to follow. Even though I was shorter than the foreman and trailing behind, I am certain I could see he was smirking, or was he gripping his pipe in his teeth as he tried not to laugh. Here I was to meet the office staff, some I managed to get on with others - not so well.

Harold Meekin, (I always thought this an unusual name) was the foreman of the shift and ultimately any disputes would be settled by him in his own style. Quite often his final words would be. "Grow up and use your loaf now bugger off and stop bothering me I have a railway to run". Harold had a grip on all the engines available, where they were and where they should be at any particular time and for which job. Were they in need of repair? The tonnage they were capable of pulling over which route, etc. Rarely did he need to ask advice and if he did, he would usually end up taking his own.

Fergie Graham, had the job of filling the rosters for the daily workings of the shed driver and fireman and often needed men for special jobs, such as holiday trains, special goods etc. He had a terrific memory. He knew all the footplate staff, the routes they could work, the times they were available and he very rarely made a mistake, if he did everyone would rag him about it for days. The main thing I remember about him was the number of cigarettes he would smoke over the course of a single shift, and he would use someone like me as a general dog's body. "Put the kettle on Scotty, nip over to the canteen and get me twenty players and a sandwich. Get this, bring that"! He rarely ever left his seat. The desks that most of the office staff used were about four-foot-high and built on a slope, like an architect would use for his drawings. This in turn necessitated the need for tall stools, and each person made sure he had their own. Woe betides anyone who did not adhere to this unspoken rule.

The phones, as I discovered, were usually manned by staff who were recovering from some malady or other as they made their way back to fitness when they would take up their normal duties. They would be succeeded by the next infirm body. Just at present there was no other body and it was my misfortune to be in the wrong place at the wrong time. Or as Ernie looked at it, the right place at the right time and I had saved him both time and effort looking for, what turned out to be a general dogsbody!

There were at least six men in the office all doing something different. Fergie, as I said before, did the rosters for footplate men to operate the mass of different trains that would pass through Carlisle every twenty-four hours, or arranging to fit into the time tables, the special excursions or special goods trains. He must have known every footplateman on the shed, or at least it seemed that way. He was aware of which routes each driver could take. Route learning was a necessity. Before a driver took a train on a route he hadn't been on before, it was imperative that he learned where all the stops were, all the timings from A to B, Signal boxes, platform layouts and countless other safety measures. Having said all that, it was always the guard on the train who was in charge. Before the start of any trip he would inform the driver of the number of carriages/goods wagons and the approximate weight of the train. The driver in turn, would tell the guard if a banker would be needed for any steep parts of the journey. (A banker was an assist engine that would give the train a boost to the top of a steep gradient.)

There was someone else arranging engines to pull the said trains, this would normally be an ex driver maybe someone who had failed his regular medical. These guys had to know their business in order to avoid any problems along the way. It was kind of an awkward job, as sometimes the engines delegated to one job or another would break down or as coaches were added to the trains they would need a different, more powerful engine. I have watched them scratching their heads, it was like playing chess; move this here, move that there, bring that one back into steam for the next shift, nick one that should be going to Glasgow and send it to Leeds as the Glasgow one wouldn't be needed for another few hours, which would be when the next shift came on and it would be then be their problem.

One man was booking on clerk. If he didn't like you, if you caused him any hassle or were a few minutes late, you would be quartered (a quarter of an hour taken from your pay.) As far as I could gather, he was also the only person on the shift with any medical knowledge. This was earned through necessity and many times I have watched as he would tend to burns, or scalds from the hot steam and there were many. Hot ash in the eye seemed to be a major problem for the men on what was known as fire dropping. (This is where the fireboxes, ash pans and smoke boxes, were cleaned and emptied after each run.) The least bit of wind would create clouds of soot and ash which, in turn, would make it difficult to see, but even worse, was trying to breathe without gasping for air. There was always the accompanied smell of sulphur, but the old guys just laughed and said it helped keep you clear of colds, I am not entirely sure about that. The only safety measure I can remember at the time, was the odd handkerchief around the lower half of the face and would make them look like bank robbers in a western film. A few of the guys on these jobs would have other jobs to go to and the sooner they could get finished, the sooner they could get away. Each engine would be allocated a certain amount of time to complete each job and it was not unusual for them to be booking off within a few hours of booking on There was never a problem with this way of working, as long as the engines were ready for their next job.

The switch board that I was expected to look after was a small box affair, it had a series of tiny light bulbs that would flash at the same time a buzzer would sound, rather like Morse code in unison to the flashing lights. Each shed had its own code and this blinking thing seemed to be constantly buzzing and flashing and I was expected, almost from the start, to recognise which lights and which buzzer was for the shed, answer properly and dutifully transfer the caller to the right person. Well, that was a laugh from the start. At first, to create a good impression with the men in the office, I would answer every light and every buzzer. Chaos is a good word and I may have invented it! I would take the calls from everywhere and blithely transfer them, not always to the right person or the right location. It was likened to Fred Carno's army. A phone call from the station master would find its way to the coaling plant, or signal box 5 would be connected to a shed in Glasgow - it may not have been funny then, but it still raises a smile when I think about it. After a short while, and many wrong numbers, Ernie decided maybe I wasn't cut out to be in the office after all, and put me to work filling the dirt wagon at the end of the shed. "That should keep you out of bother," were his parting words, or maybe they were what I heard, as he clenched his pipe in his teeth, disappearing in a cloud of St. Bruno smoke.

The dirt wagon turned out to be a meeting point for all the cleaners and passed cleaners, so I always had company. However the same lads could disappear, like a puff of smoke, when any bosses appeared. But most of the lads were decent and would lend a hand showing me how it was done, and I wasn't averse to asking them to show me one more time, mostly they told me what I could do and duly returned my shovel, telling me where it could be put!

At sixteen years of age nothing seemed to faze any of the lads I worked with, or maybe it was mostly bravado! It was an established theme on the railway that when you finished the job you had been designated, you could go home. I am sure the bosses at head office knew this happened, but as long as the job got done I don't think they cared.

The best job for allowing an early finish was fire dropping and at times, the fire droppers seemed to no sooner book on until they were booking off again, having completed their quota of engines. Without doubt these jobs were never done as they should have been. The corners of the firebox were almost a part of something else and could be left with amazing amounts of clinker and ash. The smoke box handles were loosened, and some ash scattered on the front of the engine in an attempt to make it look as if the smoke box had been cleaned and emptied as it should have been. Anything to speed up the job, to make it look as if all the work had been completed and allow the fire droppers to get finished and be off home, or in a lot of cases to their second job. This was possibly the dirtiest job on the shed, a close second was steam raising. However, when asked to do any of these jobs at busy times, a few of us jumped at the chance while many of the lads would sooner skive off and play cards or in some cases disappear to the pictures. I don't for one minute think that the bosses were unaware of what went on, I think it was just easier for them to ignore the situation. In my case, not only did I get to go home early but received labourers pay into the bargain, a double bonus.

During a night time shift and while waiting for engines to arrive I became a little bit bored. I had found a dead bird on the smoke box on one of the engines and had set it to one side. A little later when everyone was busy, I retrieved it with great stealth, and shoved it in the oven above the stove (These types of stoves seemed to feature in every bothy on British Rail.) Quietly as possible I closed the door. I must admit that I didn't know that one of the guys had put a pie in the self-same oven to have a little later when he got a break. I don't have to tell anyone the whole outcome, but I was not welcome on that shift for some time. The guy with the pie used some words completely new to me however, I did recognise the few that meant me becoming a corpse.

These men did have difficult and, not to put too fine a point on it, extremely dangerous jobs. They had to contend with hot ashes and burning coal, scalding steam and above all a hundred tons of red hot steel above their heads. A lot of the time, in fact most of the time, these great engines were parked over the ash pits without their hand brakes on, totally out of order but it did make it easier and avoided climbing on and off each footplate every time, simply to put on the hand brake and then to release it half an hour later. This way, by climbing on to the rear engine, it was possible to push the whole gaggle of engines forward as soon as the fire droppers had finished the task as each engine was moved with more than likely, a young cleaner in unofficial charge of the manoeuvre. Risk assessment - don't make me laugh!

It always appeared to me that some of the fire droppers came to work almost as they had left it the previous day, still with ash on their clothing and hardly a sign that even their faces had seen water since the last shift. Maybe that is why the bait cabin they used always had a sour smell of sweat, and unwashed sweat at that. I know that very few people at that time had a bath in their homes, but most of us could manage a wash over the kitchen sink. Some of the fire droppers were a little more fastidious and with a bit of Mackie's soft soap from the bucket, a piece of cotton waste to block the plug hole and an endless supply of hot water, they would strip to the waist and give themselves a well-deserved wash down.

Maybe I am being a little bit harsh on these guys because, by-and-large, they were a good crew and kind hearted, willing to help with any problem and would give a hand where needed. This without doubt, was one of the most dangerous jobs on the shed and they earned every penny they made. As a permanent job I don't think I would have had the right mind set or the stamina to keep it up month after month. But in those days it was part of life for a lot of people, many who never thought of changing their job, it was a common saying as I remember. Better the devil you know!

CHAPTER 21

Over the years when asked directions to this place or that, where possible, I have tended to use pubs as landmarks. But over the last decade or so it is becoming increasingly difficult, almost overnight these local hostelries are closing their doors as it becomes harder for the owners to make a living. I wonder what my old mentors from my railway days would think. If it had been mentioned to some of them in those misty days of yore, that more than half of the pubs they frequented as footplate men would be closed, and in some cases demolished to make room for houses, I bet they would have had quite a few unsavoury remarks to make as they supped their light and dark or their nut brown. After all, in a lot of cases these meeting places were the life blood of communities were they not? There wouldn't be anyone foolish enough or have the nerve to close such places, would they? These hostelries were also the trade mark meeting places for rail men as they gathered for a quick half before booking on. Or a little more after booking off.

Each shed was blessed with a nearby public house and it always proved useful when arranging to meet before a shift or if a fireman or driver went on loan to another shed or were on a booking off trip. But I can't remember any footplate man ever needing an excuse to visit one or other of these meeting places, after all these places were on a par to institutions at least.

Wherever I visited during the time I worked on the railway, there was always the aficionado on beer who wasn't found wanting in informing all how good or bad the ale was at any pub they visited. Some of the pubs would develop a name other than its given name, such as The Caledonian in Carlisle known amongst local railwaymen as The Cally or Platform Nine. Normal everyday folk visiting the said pub for a drink could have been in fear of being run down by a train, such were the discussions between drivers and firemen, and not forgetting the guards. Good God, don't forget the guards! After all the guards were always in charge of the train not, as some might think, the driver. The guard was always in the right and never short of making his position quite clear and telling everyone at every opportunity.

The crash of dominoes or the thud of darts in the board, were a constant accompaniment to the chatter about trains, times, engines and so on and the ribaldry amongst rival sheds was always added to the mix. Almost always good natured, but now and again tempers could flare up along with some questionable language. There was never any background music and I am sure it wouldn't have been allowed to interfere with the major discussions taking place in the comfort of the bar and its surroundings. Nor was there any band or group playing on a stage. These places were for drinking and communication with all the like- minded railwaymen.

The mindset of that time was, if they wanted to listen to music, there was the railway club or the ex- servicemen's club or one of the other many clubs around the town.

I am sure that visitors from away would wonder just what language was being used and from which country. The drink would take hold and the Cumbrian or worse, the local dialect, would pop its head up over the counter. It makes me wonder how these places have taken such a back seat when they were so alive not that long ago, and it was all free, apart from the drink.

CHAPTER 22

As young lads on night shift and of course with all our work done, some of us would slip away, (at least those with a few pennies to spare would). Up through Kingmoor Wood to the old A6 at Kingstown, where we would find the Aero café. None of us knew why it was called the Aero café until we had been making visits over a few months. We were then informed by a local know it all. "You lot must be thick! Don't you know that just over the road used to be an airfield?" Well how thick can one get?

During one of our escapades to the said Aero, pushing our way through the bushes and the brambles in the dark, some wise arse in a very loud voice asked "what the hell is that?" For a moment everyone stood still trying to locate just what he was eluding to. "There man! In the bushes - are you all blind." He was right, there in the bushes was a large white unidentifiable shape and it was heading toward this little group of fearless teenagers! "Maybe it's the foreman," someone whispered. "It's a bloody ghost," was the next comment. Without waiting to find an explanation, he was off like a bolting bunny with the rest of the crew hard on his heels. For some reason, I kept looking back and it suddenly dawned on me it was simply a cow, and it was as interested as we were to find out what was causing all the noise. Even though I now knew what this ghost was and I shouted as loud as I could "What are you all running for? It's only a bloody old cow." I was at the same time breaking world records in the hundred-yard dash, overtaking most of my pals, I still couldn't stop myself running. Something had hold of my mind and the adrenaline was running through my veins, it was impossible to stop. My breath was coming in sobs now, but still I tried to get everyone to stop. Fast though we were, the cow was obviously gaining ground, making short work of the brambles that were intent on bringing our flight to a halt. The street light on the main road gave us a little light to see, but it did the same for this curious cow. There was no slowing down, a wire fence, obviously put in our way deliberately, was not much of an obstacle after the tearing brambles and not just a few nettles. I think the cow knew about the fence and came to a halt to watch, as bodies tipped, jumped and attempted to dive, over the wire. We can't have been that interesting as the pursuer simply flicked her tail and decided to look for more interesting quarry. It turned out, after getting our breath back, that none of the group was frightened or in the least concerned about our flight, in fact everyone knew what they were running from and were just having a laugh. I can't remember anyone going to the Aero for the next few weeks or months as everyone seemed too busy or had no money or....!

From a passed cleaner upwards, everyone involved on the footplate was duty bound to look at the rosters, which were posted daily. They were known as the links. They had the name of the driver and fireman, along with time and destination of all the trains, with all the Kingmoor staff and always gave an indication of seniority among drivers, passed firemen and firemen. Dragging along at the bottom were, of course, us lowly passed cleaners all trying to be men, when most of us were still teenagers. The newly passed cleaners were usually first in the booking office. Maybe today would be lucky for someone but to be fair, most of us eventually got a turn at being firemen for the day. And it all counted! When a certain number firing turns, as they were known, was reached, one would step up to a new pay grade and qualify to go on the main line, great stuff. As I lived a long way from the engine shed, it was sometimes impossible for them to contact me for a job and it would be allocated to the next person in line. But it was ok for me to claim the said turn and add it to my accumulative total to gain my stripes as it were, and join the big lads on the main line. But the rule was only the turn would be granted and not the remuneration, always a catch but the numbers added up.

As weeks went by I was given more and more firing turns, but these were only local trips from shed to shed or marshalling yard to marshalling yard, hauling trains with various goods wagons, where they would be reassembled and eventually sent off to various towns and cities around Britain. At this time a new marshalling yard was being built and was going to be the largest in Europe when it was eventually completed. Even though its design and the way it was to be built were right at the time it started, it was never to be fully utilized. As ballast and slag was required for this mammoth task, all the materials had to be brought to the site by train and many new jobs were created for the staff at Kingmoor.

Many times as a passed cleaner, my name would come up on the roster board as fireman for this or that ballast train to and from Merry Gill Quarry at Warcop or a trip to Workington for a train load of coal pit slag. Not very prestigious but all counted for my future. How times change, some of these lines were already in line to be closed by the dreaded hatchet man, Beeching. As a man he was probably the most hated person ever to work on the railway, if not in the whole of Britain.

The part I was waiting for was the chance to become the footplate crew heading off to all the places with names I had heard of but had never been to. Names banded about in the bothy - Glasgow, Hellifield, Leeds, Sheffield up the long drag, or over the top at Beattock. All places heard about, but to me they could have been in foreign countries for all I knew. For now, it was up and down from one place to another but all in the confines of the great border city Carlisle. What I didn't realise, this was all part of becoming a fireman, practice and experience, how to keep a head of steam, how to make sure the boiler was full, was there enough water in the tank or do we need to fill up at the next stop. Every time I stepped up on the footplate I learned something new. How, and why, to keep the footplate itself clean and tidy, how to pull the coal forward, all knowledge being built in my memory. Some drivers explained why this or why that, but there was some proper ar**s that would take delight in letting you sort it all out by yourself before ranting and raving. Expressions such as "are you bloody stupid have you learned nothing, what makes you think you will make a bloody fireman? You would be hard pushed to keep the fire on in the grate at home! Here, give me that bloody shovel and watch because I won't show you again." But they were in the minority. Most drivers were very good and wouldn't see anyone stuck, they would lend a hand at the water tower or at the coaling plant. They were great, but somehow it is the intolerant ones I seem to remember most.

One episode I recall, a certain driver, at this point I will call Jimmy was so horrible and un-helpful, I doubt if he even liked himself. (The crack was that he was taken off the passenger link when he failed his medical for one reason or another and confined to local working. It didn't go down very well with him and he tended to take it out of any and every one.) While on duty on the station shunt early afternoon, I needed some cigarettes - I could have got them before signing on, but as we were going to be in the station for the whole shift I didn't think it would be a problem. Would he let me leave the footplate and get some at the paper stall on platform four? Would he hell as like. "You should have got them before you signed on, wait until end of the shift." That was that. After steam heating a couple of carriages to be attached to a Glasgow express, the guard came to the footplate to give Jimmy some instructions and before he left I asked if he could get me the fags. He looked across at my driver, Jimmy didn't speak. "No problem" he replied. I handed him the money to pay for them and looked over at my driver again, I could see there was no love lost between the two. Jimmy was scowling and looked as if he was chewing a wasp. The rest of the time I spent with this driver I never offered to do anything more than was my job.

These magnificent pieces of engineering which could pull hundreds of tons of freight and/or passenger carriages, were bereft of any basic amenities, no lavatory, no way of making tea not even anywhere to wash, just a bucket. At the end of a shift the only way for a wash was to put the steam pipe, used for keeping the floor clean, into the bucket and by adjusting the pressure with the brass tap it was possible to get some hot water. After half an hour or so, it was possible to use the water that hadn't spilled with the rock and rolling on the footplate, to remove some of the grime on hands and face. But maybe on reflection, it would have been better to leave the soot and the dust until getting home as the Panda effect around the eyes and mouth always brought a smile to any passers-by met outside the station, maybe the look would have been better kept for Halloween. Although thinking back it isn't everyone that can say they have washed their faces with water from a railway engine boiler!

During my formative years as a cleaner I was often press ganged into doing labourers jobs, although like most of my peer's I would make great play of trying to avoid being drawn into the greater scheme of things, but was as happy as a sand boy to be given the opportunity to earn a few extra pounds - unaware at the time that all the things I was doing would have a bearing on my future. Called on to do fire dropping, shed sweeping etc. there was one job that I hated - tube cleaning. This work entailed being wrapped up like a Mummy and using a high-pressure airline connected to a lance. This would blow all the ash from the tubes. (At least that was the theory.) The tubes were designed to allow the heat from the firebox through to the smoke box where, on route, it would heat the water in the boiler. When the ash blocked the tubes it reduced the efficiency of the engine and so, had to be removed. This was the only job I came across where there were any concessions made to the wellbeing of the person designated to the task. A metal mask was provided, together with a material resembling a piece of bandage stuck to a thin layer of cotton wool. Today, it would give the mask Hannibal Lecter was forced to wear, a good run for design. The upside of this job was, when I had completed two or three engines I could sign off and go home and collect more than double the wage of a passed cleaner. And let's face it money was a scarce resource for a young lad, and no matter how much the wage packet had in it on a Friday, it was never quite enough. So every opportunity to earn a little more was taken - even tube cleaning. Being black as a coalman never bothered me, but my mam always had something to say about the mess I made of her clean towels. "Don't they have soap and water at that shed?" Was one of her particular favourites she used from time to time, but I am sure she knew that what she was saying was water off a duck's back. No pun intended!

CHAPTER 23

The suit I had acquired for my brother's wedding was to become invaluable over the coming years. It must have been an age thing, girls had become a source of interest not only to me, but to all my pals. Now local dances were also interesting, not so much the dancing, as the girls that did the dancing. A group of us would make plans to meet up, mostly in one pub or another. (Well, *always* in one pub or another.) After a couple of pints of Dutch courage we would sally forth to the Cosmo, the Cameo, the County or the Mitre, depending on which was the nearest. Whichever one we went to, there was always a queue and this would give us a chance to view the talent before going inside. Once through the door, all the boys would congregate at one end of the dance floor while the girls took up position at the other. Some of the older lads had regular girlfriends, but would always plan to meet inside the dancehall as it would save a few bob on the tickets. Most of us were smart, in fact some of us thought we were the dog's bollocks so to speak, nice suit, polished winkle picker shoes, various cuts to the suit. Drain pipes were on their way in, as was teddy boy attire. Pale blue, grey or even pink material, pockets and collars edged with different colours of velvet but usually black. Hair well-greased, accompanied by the requisite DA cut (Ducks Arse)! Almost always a comb, kept in the breast pocket and always in need of a good wash, but what the hell. (This was a requirement to keep the hair just right and used at every opportunity, a mirror was not needed, a shop window would do.) At the bottom of the skin-tight trousers were of course, the suede shoes or brothel creepers as they were commonly known. Very comfortable, but in the rain the soles sounded as if there were dish cloths attached to each foot with a loud squelch given off at each step. Another new vogue was just arriving luminous socks and boy, were they luminous. But usually ventured into by the real teds.

None of us had a clue about dancing. In fact up until that time, we avoided it as if it wasn't macho enough, but now it was different. Girls were becoming more and more interesting. At about the same time, my older sister would often remark "You will never click if you don't know how to dance". She would try and persuade me to learn and offered to show me how. But as a teenager I was difficult to persuade, the odd time she would take my hands and do a few steps with me to show how easy it was. The only record we had that was in fashion at that time, was Vic Damone's – On the Street Where You Live – and it was played to death. If I thought there was none of the family about I would allow Mary to cajole me into doing a little practice – it would be totally out of order otherwise. My sister and her pals would go to the local dances every week then, and if we had had a couple of pints and were at the same venue, her pals would insist that we joined in. That is how I learned how to dance the waltz, the quick step, and a bit of jive.

It was about this time I met my first date. I had been sent to Durranhill shed to help coal some engines, one of the men booked to do the job hadn't turned in. I was happy to do it as it meant more money in my wages, although I made a bit of a fuss, for appearance sake and for anyone who happened to be listening to let them know it was, at least, under a little duress.

Having caught the C4 bus into the town centre I now needed to change to get to Durranhill. There was a bus standing outside Studholmes at the Town Hall and without thinking, I had assumed it would get me to where I needed to be and hopped aboard. Downstairs was almost full, but I got a window seat near the front. Busy looking at the passing shops as we pulled away from the stop, I felt someone sit down in the seat beside me turning my head, as you do, there was a nice-looking girl right next to me. (Unlike today when it is not considered P/C), she said "Hello, off to work then?" It was an obvious but nice introduction. Before I could answer she followed up with, "On the railway I see." Good observation again. My mouth opened to reply but the words didn't get spoken. Tongue tied, taken aback, or both.

"My dad's on the railway, he is a driver at Upperby. That's how I recognised the uniform."

Before she could say anymore and as she caught her breath, I said, "I'm just on my way to Durranhill to coal some engines." As if she would know about that.

She gave a little laugh." Not on this bus I hope, this bus goes to Currock."

I almost said "Bloody hell", but instead I muttered. "If you let me past I need to get the right bus."

"You can get off at St. Nicolas and catch the right one from there."

She swung her legs into the aisle to let me by.

"You from Carlisle then?"

"No – Wigton." I replied, as I squeezed past.

"Do you go to the dances then? We go to the County on Saturday nights, me and my friends. Be nice to see you if you get there."

"I'll see what the lads are doing first, depends on the shifts."

As I reached the back of the bus she called out. "My name is Jean, just in case you make it on Saturday, good luck with the right bus."

What a clown I felt and her attractive, smartly dressed, it could only happen when I had made a right fool of myself. I managed the right bus, but couldn't get the girl out of my mind. However, she slipped from my thoughts as I spent the next few hours shovelling coal.

Jean was, however, to appear on the scene on the following Saturday night. Using a little bit of subterfuge and a bit of underhand persuading, I managed to cajole some of the team to venture to the County ballroom as it was called a nice venue. We had to queue almost around the building to get in, and one or two were for giving up and heading elsewhere. After a bit of humming and ahhing! We were half way up the stairs and decided to stay.

They hadn't realised yet, my ulterior motive but would be very vocal when they did.

A pint in the bar downstairs and then up to the dance floor. I didn't realise how difficult it would be to try and look uninterested in the girls as they sat around the edge of the dance floor. But my head was dizzy as my eyes tried to search out the reason I had for coming here.

Not a sign. I stood with my back to the band and almost willed everyone to stand still a minute, until I could see if this girl had decided to come here, or go on to one of the other dances in the town.

This may sound scripted, but believe me it wasn't. A slight touch on my shoulder, and thinking it was one of the lads I said "not now."

There it was again, that light touch on my shoulder. I turned with the start of a swear word or two on my lips. There she was dressed like a film star and looking straight at me! No one else - Me!

She was with a couple of other girls, but as the band was playing I never heard the introductions. She leaned on my shoulder like an old friend and, more shouted than spoke in my ear "I didn't think you had heard me and if you had I didn't think you would come!"

What should I say next? I could talk easily to my pals, but this approach had me speechless. I didn't say anything because before any thoughts could be turned into words. "Hey Scotty, what's this then? You trying to keep these all to yourself?"

I should have known. Threlk (nick name) had burst onto the scene. "No wonder you wanted to come here. Go on then, are you going to introduce us?"

The other two of our group had now joined in. "Dark horse Scotty, or what, you never said anything about meeting girls, very sneaky if you ask me."

CHAPTER 24

The steam almost blew the waiting passengers from the platform. Well, not quite, because the steam cocks were pointed towards the ground. But it happened every-time we were to leave the platform, the driver had to clear any water in the cylinders and it wasn't deliberate, the only way was to open the cocks before opening the regulator. It always brought a smile to my face and I think to the drivers face as well, the people on the platform, waving goodbye to their loved ones, almost always jumped a mile as the steam escaped. And with a heavy train the wheels would spin and cause no end of consternation. Today was my first official job on the main line working a passenger train. The engine hauling our train was quite unusual in that it was as clean as a new pin, sparkling in its British Rail green with gold coach lines and numbers, a beautiful Clan class. I am not sure if it was as clean as it was because it had just come from the workshops, or maybe it was because it was to commemorate my first job as fireman on a passenger train. I would like to think the latter, but have a sneaking suspicion in may have been the former!

As the driver closed the steam cocks and the great driving wheels settled down, after being allowed to show off a little, the steel of the wheels bit the steel rails, the massive engine eased the coaches on their journey. The train was bound for Leeds over the Midland line and it was my job to see there was enough water in the boiler and make sure there was the required steam pressure at all times, keep the fire right, which, at that particular moment, was on a par with a view of Dantes Hell, white hot, turning coal into living flames instantly. Directing the coal with the shovel was in itself an art. Using the fire shovel pointed through the Firehole to see where coal was needed, soon became second nature, and the feeling of being able to put the fuel just where it was needed was indeed a skill and eventually even I would be able to get it right.

It isn't possible to transfer the feeling of a young lad being in this position, damp rag in hand taking the fire shovel and putting the coal where it was needed in the firebox, the plumes of dark smoke exuding from the funnel and managing to fill the cab, as we headed from the station.

The engine was roaring now it seemed happy it was being allowed to get on and do the job it was meant to. Over the points and the engine lurched one way, the tender holding the coal and water to keep the beast going lurched the other. Me with one foot on the tender and the other on the cab floor was something else, I had learned a lot on the goods trains where I had been fireman and it stood me in good stead. My driver looked across, his expression said what was needed to be said and without a word, a slight lift of his head and a little smile asked "OK!" As he wound back the gearing and the engine changed its beat as it took the weight of the carriages in its stride. I remember seeing the signalman looking from his perch in the box, probably making sure we were on time leaving the Citadel.

We were already out of Carlisle, houses, gardens and fields, passed by faster and faster as we picked up speed hurrying up the line. The noise we were creating increased dramatically as we clattered through the various stations along the line, the tiddly dum, tiddly dum, tiddly dum, interrupted by the wheels feeling the points and the shorter joints, losing the steady rhythm for few minutes until we were clear of the station.

This first passenger journey had no problems and, to other firemen would not have rated as anything other than another trip, but to me, this was the journey, this was the trip that would stay with me the rest of my life. Many other journeys would be more dramatic, more hilarious, or more couldn't care less, but none would be so memorable.

The first twenty or so miles were, as I remember, comparatively easy, through Armathwaite, Lazonby and on to Appleby. The next section was where the engine needed to get the bit between her teeth, as did I. I don't really recollect the following place names as my back was never straight, my mind and my eyes jumped from steam gauge to the boiler water gauge to firebox, with fire shovel hardly leaving my hand.

There weren't many fat firemen on the railway at that time and after this trip I would understand why. This was truly earning a living with the sweat from my brow.

The driver touched me on the shoulder and half shouted in my ear, "You can take it easy for now - we're ower t top." I half nodded to acknowledge his gesture, before pushing the shovel into the coal in the tender, followed by the biggest stretch of my back I can ever remember. I am sure that half the coal I shovelled into the firebox came right out of the funnel, the engine had been working that hard. By the end of the journey I must have shovelled between three and four tons of coal and turned many hundreds, if not thousands, of gallons of water into steam. Some of the steam and the gas from the firebox almost choked my driver and me as we thundered through Blea Moor tunnel. Maybe I shouldn't have put such a big fire on before we entered, but I would learn all these sorts of requirements as time passed.

Hellifield station, "Well this is it lad." I was informed, as the train came to a halt at the platform. "Make sure you have all your gear or you will never see it again." He spoke in rather a loud voice as the relief crew climbed on board. The relief driver simply muttered "Cheeky bugger," or words to that effect. This was real railway banter, hardly ever said with any malice. They were both smiling as they exchanged pleasantries and imparted any information needed. As I stepped down from the footplate, the fireman nodded in my direction as he picked up the shovel to continue what I had been doing for the last seventy miles or so.

Many times over the years that fortunately, were still over the horizon, I felt kind of let down. On arrival at our destination I didn't feel elated, or happy, that we had arrived. It was more an anti-climax, pulling into a dreary goods yard, especially on a cold winter night when it was probably raining. The wagons uncoupled from the engine and the oil lamps relocated to indicate we were now a light engine and not a train. And we still had to get to the shed to dispose of the engine. Bringing the train to a stop in a station to be relieved by another crew, the station was inevitably sooty and dark usual, lit with one-watt lamps that were in desperate need of a good clean. The end of another journey and would always include the voice of the unfathomable message about the arrival and departure of the said train, the words meaning little or nothing to the travellers on the platform, or to other railway staff for that matter, these announcers had to have had very special training for them all to sound the same, unintelligible!

With the preparation of the engine I enjoyed the banter with driver and other footplate men on the shed, I nearly always felt kind of let down at the end of a trip somehow. Leaving the goods yard or the passenger station there was something to work for. The engine fighting for a foothold on the steel rails, the injectors working overtime to keep the boiler filled, the intense light from the open firebox bringing life to the surroundings of the cab. Knowing where we were bound for and all still to work for. Sometimes a doddle, sometimes a bit of a bitch. But going there and getting there were worlds apart.

It was difficult to imagine that although none of us were of the legal age to drink, it was accepted that as footplate staff we just did. Over the next few years, those of us who had started this journey together on the railway, a pattern was gradually built up. Whenever shifts allowed, a group of us would meet, mainly on a Saturday night in one pub or another and after a couple of pints would decide on a dance venue for the night. Maybe it would be Keswick or Maryport or some place a little nearer, perhaps The Cameo in Carlisle, or wherever. During the evening, the crack would eventually turn to work, and what did anyone think about a move from our local shed to somewhere more exciting. Manchester maybe or some bright spark mentioned London. What a great idea was the general consensus! Maybe we could all go to the same shed, there was never any consideration that we could all finish up at different locations.

It was at the time quite easy to transfer to another shed, always providing you had the required seniority. This was always a big thing on the railway and probably still is. From time to time there would be a notice posted in the booking on area, this would have all the information about Drivers wanted at one shed or another, firemen wanted here or there. The shed would be named along with the date of the seniority required for the position.

One time there were several vacancies at Willesden and Nine Elms in north London and the information was passed to one another like quicksilver. But not to me as I was on the wrong shifts so didn't see the vacancy list. I didn't find out until the weekend when we met up in the Caledonian bar. (More commonly referred to as the Cally.) The lads were all animated with excitement, "well I've already put in my application", was the first remark I heard. "Hang on a minute" I butted in "what's going on, what bloody application?" This was how I got to know about the transfer notice. It turned out that three of our group had already filled in a transfer form and there were only four firemen wanted. Well there was nothing to do until Monday so we decided to stay in Carlisle for the rest of the night. We could have been anywhere but there were only three topics to be discussed. London, London and London. The excitement was electric! Everyone talked over one another, how different it would be, we could go down Soho every weekend, suddenly Soho became the conversation, what a place for a group of young lads, we wouldn't need the world. Soho would be our Oyster. Then it dawned! what if none of us had the seniority because after all, seniority was the key factor. What if our transfers weren't accepted. We hadn't thought this thing through. There would be other lads at other sheds probably drawn to the bright lights of the big city wouldn't there? The excitement took over again; "No don't worry, we are bound to get whatever transfers there are, aren't we!"

We were of course wrong! Only two got the notification that they had been accepted as they had the right seniority - there was that monster again - seniority! That wasn't the case for me because on Monday, when I booked on, the list had been taken down, and when I enquired at the office it turned out that Sunday had been the cut off day for applications. So I would have to wait for the next list - whenever that might be.

It was difficult not to be caught up in the excitement of my friends who had been lucky enough to get the move, and the feeling of missing out on this great adventure. There was to be no great delay in their departure and within a couple of weeks or so they were off. No big send off, just a few pints in the Cally, then they were gone. No knowing when we would meet up, but we would meet up again of that I was sure.

Weeks passed and the going of friends dimmed as work went on, there was no such thing as keeping in touch. Hardly anyone in those far-off days had such a thing as a telephone at home – let alone a mobile, and there was never a thought about writing letters. Young lads had more to do and not enough time to write letters.

Sometimes on local work, (these were called local trips taking carriages or goods trains from yard to yard), there never seemed to be any hurry on these jobs, no need for constant watching the steam gauge or making sure we had enough water. My mind would slip back to days of my childhood.

The job I was doing reminded me of my dad's job at the Gas works. He was a stoker and he, like me, (or should that be me like him), was required to keep an eye on the way the fires were controlled. Whereas I had only one to look after, my dad had at least a dozen or so.

The main fires that kept everything going were situated below ground with access a little bit dangerous, to say the least. First, about half a dozen large metal sheets had to be moved to one side, this by itself was no mean feat. However my dad, who was as strong as an ox, although not massively built, would simply prise one of the steel sheets off the ground with the edge of his shovel and brute strength would do the rest. The ancient metal ladders were something to behold. The frame held in place with huge bolts while the steps, all bent and buckled, were not at all inviting and a certain amount of skill was required to descend and even more skill to climb back from that deep forbidding hole. With only an eerie flicker of light from the furnaces to show the way down, once down in the depths the water was inches deep on the floor. Water that was used to dampen the ashes gleaned from the white-hot retorts. Ash had to be cleaned from the grates on a regular basis and hot ash that spilled from the barrow would send up great clouds of steam and ash. This would have been a great place for a Sauna if there had been such things. (We only had a galvanised bath that hung in the kitchen until needed, never mind a sauna.)

The times and acceptance of things in those far distant days was different to now, and my dad would hardly give a thought that it might be dangerous for his son to accompany him into the depths except for his warning: "Mind where you put your feet it's slippery down here." I can't say I was ever frightened, maybe a little hesitant first time, but I had complete trust in the man down the hole, he was my dad, and he would never allow anything to happen to his best worker.

Beneath the great steel sheets, it was a different world and as the clay used to seal the furnace was removed the flicker of light became more intense. The door always reluctant to give away its hidden secrets, had to be prised open with a steel bar, the intensity of the light from the fire released at that second was blinding and the sudden blast of heat was awesome! Dad always said it would burn the skin off a rice pudding. But I must admit I was never to let on to my mother that I was allowed to help dad under those great steel sheets. I wonder why?

These great retorts would gobble up anything in seconds, and God knows what, one time or another, would meet its end there. All types of dead animals were disposed of, dead farm animals, dogs, cats that had come to the end of their lives, they would all go to meet their maker in one or other of these infernos. A mere second or two and they were gone forever.

With the two lads going off to Willesden, it had sort of split up our group and we saw less of each other. Although one benefit – I just happened to see more of my new friend Jean. We went out a few times mainly to the dances or the cinema. After a few weeks Jean spent most of the time in the dance hall persuading me to come to her house for tea, "Go on you'll like mam and dad. You know he's a driver and you'll have lots in common". As the night wore on I eventually agreed. She was as happy as a sand boy.

The she came up with the idea: "As tomorrow is Sunday you could come tomorrow".

"Can't tomorrow, I'm at work." I wasn't, I just said it to give myself a breathing space, time to think this thing through – it was becoming a bit serious!

CHAPTER 25

At the end of each shift, all the footplate staff at the shed were required to look at the rosters to find out what their duties were for the following day. I had, over the last week or so, booked off at the station instead of the shed. Today I was back at Kingmoor looking for my next job, having scanned the rosters I continued along the wall and there it was! The transfer sheet with all the details of what was available. Eyes running down the names of the sheds with vacancies: two firemen wanted at Birmingham - no good, one fireman wanted at Leeds- no good. The last shed on the list was where I wanted to be, for no other reason than that is where my pals had gone. Three firemen wanted at Willesden! My seniority fitted the dates required. Excitement was sending little shivers down my back. Same procedure as last time I went right to the booking office and asked for the relevant information. "What do you want to leave here for? I was just getting used to your cheeky face." I suppose he was entitled to ask as I had got to know him quite well, having been in the office on the phones and running back and forth on the company bike to knock up drivers and firemen on special occasions. But at this moment I just couldn't wait. "Come on Joe can I please have a form?" It must have looked as though my life depended on having a form. Shaking his head from side to side he left the window to retrieve a form. As he handed it to me he had to let me know. "Mark my words you will regret it. They are not like us down there you know."

I was given the form to fill in, I am sure I filled it in with pencil, double checking that all the questions were answered, and asked the booking clerk who I should give it to. Putting his hand through the peep hole he told me he would do it for me, as it had to be in the following day.

Was this it? Would my application go through? Would I be pipped at the post by someone with greater seniority?

It was now in the lap of the Gods, or maybe a railway official or two. Only time would tell. I wasn't sure how I would broach the subject with my mam, I knew dad would be alright, at least I felt sure he would be ok with my going to London. Better put it off until I found out if it was going to happen. I hadn't told anyone in the family last time so it would be better to wait.

Shift after shift went by. Didn't they want me – an experienced fireman? Well, only a passed cleaner really, but that was just splitting hairs, I had been doing the job for ages now, I still had a lot to learn but that was by the by.

I had just booked on when the clerk shouted me back, "Here lad this is for you," and handed me a brown envelope. The words emblazoned on the front "George Scott number 589 passed cleaner". I was about to open it when that awful feeling came over me, maybe I have missed out again, what if this, or what if that. What the hell I obliterated the envelope as the booking clerk watched, half a smile on his lips. The letter had my name same as the envelope and a few short words underneath. I haven't got it again, went through my mind before it dawned on me the words read: "You are required to report at Willesden Motive Power Depot on Monday, the letter included the date and the time".

"I have to read it again", went through my head. I couldn't believe it. I leaned through the window without a second thought. "Who do I see about this?" pointing to the letter in my hand. "Transfer?" Was all the clerk asked. "Yeh, Yeh! To Willesden." I blurted. "A week on Monday." "Pop up and see them in the main office," he remarked, as he slid the window closed. I was off like a Greyhound before anyone could change their mind – I had to make sure.

The office manager was ok, maybe a little offhand, although he must have done this transfer lark many times. I still thought he was not giving me his full attention and was about to put him right, when he turned back to face me. The look on his face told me not to say anything at all. He explained everything. "Come back on Wednesday, we will have your travel pass and a temporary place for you to stay after that it will be up to you."

Well I had done it! I had certainly done it this time – no going back now. My going to London filled me with great excitement. My biggest worry was how to tell my mam. As far as she was concerned I had forgotten all about leaving home and going off to London. That, to my mam, was a far-away place. It could even be foreign!

I was obsessed for the next days trying to work just how to tell her. She would go mad if I told her that I had asked for a transfer! She would go mad if I told her I wanted to go. The devil was in when, and what, I told her. It would have to be as near the day of departure, but giving me time to buy some gear to take with me without raising any suspicion. Mams being mams, there was no hiding anything from a mam. I should have known! She had, after all, brought up five of us and was as wise as any mam could be.

I tried everything to avoid too much conversation or contact with any of the family. It didn't work and my dad was the first to say anything. "Are you in trouble lad?" I nearly jumped out of my skin when he asked. My answer was a bit short, on reflection, "No. What would be the matter?" "Hey lad I'm your dad, don't take that tone with me. I'll ask again, what is the problem? Even your mam has noticed. Come on the longer you bottle it up the worse it will be."

I had no choice, I had to come clean and brought him up to date with everything. All the while trying not to sound too excited. "When were you going to tell us?" He asked, after I had spilled the beans.

"Well, I was waiting until as close to the day as possible so mam wouldn't be to upset and try to persuade me not to go. You know how good she is at that sort of thing."

"You are right about one thing – she is upset! And I think you had better tell her as soon as she comes in, don't you?" I thought about it for about a second nodded my agreement. "As soon as I see her." I promised.

Mam never cried, at least not when anyone was around, it was not the thing to do. When I told her about London her eyes filled up, she breathed deeply to hold back the tears and her voice sounded different. "Lad, lad after all we've been through to get you grown up, after all the times you've been ill, what makes you want to leave home and go to London of all places?"

At first, I tried the line that it was my job and they wanted me to go. But she saw through that, maybe I should try the route that I wasn't going for good. That didn't work. "If you aren't going for good why are you going at all?" Cornered, I had to give in and tell all. Dad, as I expected, hadn't much to say at that moment but I suspect he had a lot to do in the background, persuading my mam that I would soon be sick and come home.

The rest of the time up to my departure was not as bad as I thought it would be and before I knew it was time to go. "Have you got everything you need? Dad get that old suitcase down off the top of the wardrobe. I'll help him pack." "Mam I am not an invalid, I can manage." Mam pretended not to have heard. "What are you taking? You better have spare trousers. Two or three shirts won't do. Your overalls will be better in a paper bag – I've washed them but you want nothing putting them in the same case as your good things." I could feel mam welling up as the day progressed, and tried to placate her but it didn't work. I was in the way and it would be a good idea to go and see my grandmother and bring her up to date. Mam didn't know, but my grandmother already knew. She was the first person I had told. I'd told her even before telling my dad.

My grandmother has a special place in my heart and will be there forever. I could tell her anything, well almost anything, she always understood. She had, however, tried to get me to tell my mother of my venture, but she had never blabbed, she had kept her own counsel and understood where I was coming from by not letting on. As always, before I could depart, my Grandmother insisted on giving me an envelope. I knew what would be inside – money! I tried to refuse it, saying she needed it more than me. But, as always, she made me take it, saying - if I didn't use it I could give her it back next time I saw her.

It was early Sunday morning when I left, and even though mam and dad were up to see me off, there were no recriminations, no last minute "don't goes." As I was going through the front door, dad squeezed my shoulders and nodded, "look after yourself lad and take care it's a big world out there." Mam took my forearm, I could see there was pleading in her eyes and I could see the tears, but she avoided saying anything - just turned and went back into the kitchen. Dad stood at the doorway and waved a couple of times as I left the avenue. When I reached the top of the street I turned for a last wave, but he was gone. The front door was closed.

On my way, the train lurched into motion as the great engine drew the red coaches away from the platform. Only one stop before my destination - three hundred miles into the future. The countryside flashed by. But unlike my first trip, I was used to the motion of the coaches mimicking the engine as she settled into her stride.

This journey was new to me, as most of my time as a fireman I had spent on routes into Scotland and over the great Midland line. Smoke and steam cascading across the adjoining fields, the little stations as they blurred past the windows were not new, they were just situated on a different line.

Crewe Station slid past the carriage window and the same garbled voice came over the loud speakers. Crowds of people shuffled in all directions, trying to make up their minds where they would get the best seats. Heading first in one direction before deciding it might be better the other end of the train. Doors slammed, the guards whistle gave a shrill blast at the back of the train, and in answer the engine acknowledged. The train slid away from the platform. Passengers were still undecided which way to head next, but in a short while had made the decision where they would park their belongings and take a seat.

As the bodies settled down, papers and magazines unfurled, pipes and cigarettes were lit, the wheels of the carriages clickity clacked over the points as the train left Crewe - next stop London.

We galloped past stations I was to get to know over the coming weeks and months - Stafford, Rugely, Rugby, Bletchley, hurtling through tunnels and clattering past goods trains on the slow lane. This wasn't new to me, after all I was a footplateman. I wondered at the time if it obvious to the other passengers. Yes - it was bound to be wasn't it?

The windows of the coach were almost sucked from their mountings as we entered the tunnel at Watford just as another express hurtled past heading north. I noticed one or two of my fellow travellers ducked at the ear popping experience, and I smiled inwardly.

Euston station - what can I say. I remembered being in awe of Glasgow but this place was something else. It resembled a great blackened colosseum. The advertising boards must have been cleaned recently and stood out from the rest of the building. Would you believe it! The largest advert, in blue and gold letters at least a couple of feet high, was for Carrs of Carlisle Cream Crackers - Biscuit manufacturers for over one hundred years. Wasn't that something? I was three hundred miles away and this was the first sign I read.

As a railwayman I couldn't look lost to my fellow travellers. However, my stomach was churning as my eyes searched for at least one of my old pals from up north. I wandered along the platform trying to find a friendly face amongst the milling crowd, all heading for the exit. There were people waiting for friends and relatives at the far end of the platform, but no sign of anyone I knew.

"They have forgotten" was a phrase that was building in my head, "they have bloody well forgotten I was coming! How will I find the Polygon club?" That was where I was supposed to be going to stay. Everyone had told me it was only a few minutes from the station, but a wrong turn could lead me miles away.

Brain now in overdrive, I was on the verge of asking at the ticket desk when I heard the voice. "Hey! Scotty ower here man, ower here." The whole train load of passengers seemed to look around to verify who this Scotty was. I dumped my old suitcase at my feet and waved through the crowd. The same voice I had just heard, gave vent again only even louder. "Away man ower here, we've been waiting for ages." This was exactly what I needed to hear. Accompanying the loud voice, one of the lads was jumping up and down waving his arms around. No excuse – me - I just barged my way across to where they were standing at the top of the ramp leading to the main concourse.

My heart kind of skipped a beat, was I pleased to see Dave and Ron. "No wonder the train was late." Ron remarked in a daft sort of way. "Did they let you be fireman?" Ha! Ha! Ha! Lots of back slapping, but no mention of a little help with my luggage.

"We're gan for a pint at the Lion and Lamb, I hope you fetched some money with you."

"A couple of quid." I replied, "anyway it's you lot that should be buying the drink."

The End

ABOUT THE AUTHOR

George lives in Cumbria with his wife Isobel and is now retired – from shovelling coal at least! He found out that he likes animals far better than people and, in his later years, set up a wildlife rescue centre. But that is a tale for another time...

The centre is a registered charity and all the proceeds from the sale of Tom Scott's Lad will be going directly to www.knoxwood.org

31757378R00087

Printed in Poland
by Amazon Fulfillment
Poland Sp. z o.o., Wrocław